continued . . .

THE PRESIDENT'S DAUGHTER

"High-tension action and harrowing twists—Higgins at his best." —*Midwest Book Review*

"A tight story with plenty of action, appealing heroes, and dastardly villains." —*Chattanooga Free Press*

"This sizzling new thriller . . . keep[s] the pages flying." —Copely News Service

NIGHT JUDGEMENT AT SINOS

"This is one you won't put down." —*The New York Times*

DRINK WITH THE DEVIL

"A most intoxicating thriller." —The Associated Press

"It is Dillon's likability and the author's adroitness in giving his character the room he needs that make Higgins's novels so readable." —*The Washington Times*

YEAR OF THE TIGER

"Higgins spins as mean a tale as Ludlum, Forsythe, or any of them." —*Philadelphia Daily News*

ANGEL OF DEATH

"Pulsing excitement . . . Higgins makes the pages fly." —*New York Daily News*

"A terrific read." —The Associated Press

"Hurdles from one thrill to the next." —*Publishers Weekly*

"The action never stops." —*San Francisco Examiner*

"A crackling good read . . . a top-drawer thriller." —*The Virginian-Pilot*

continued . . .

MIDNIGHT MAN
Also published as *Eye of the Storm*

"Heart-stopping . . . spectacular and surprising."
—*Abilene Reporter-News*

"A riveting story . . . as current as today's headlines."
—*The Columbia (SC) State*

"Razor-edged . . . will give you an adrenaline high. It's a winner."
—*Tulsa World*

"Will leave readers happily breathless." *Kirkus Reviews*

ON DANGEROUS GROUND
"A whirlwind of action, with a hero who can out Bond old James. It's told in the author's best style, with never a pause for breath." —*The New York Times Book Review*

"A powerhouse tale of action and adventure."
—*The Tampa Tribune*

SHEBA
"When it comes to thriller writers, one name stands well above the crowd—Jack Higgins." —The Associated Press

THUNDER POINT
"Dramatic . . . authentic . . . one of the author's best."
—*The New York Times*

"A rollicking adventure that twists and turns."
—*The San Diego Union-Tribune*

Titles by Jack Higgins

EDGE OF DANGER
DAY OF RECKONING
THE WHITE HOUSE CONNECTION
IN THE HOUR BEFORE MIDNIGHT
EAST OF DESOLATION
THE PRESIDENT'S DAUGHTER
PAY THE DEVIL
FLIGHT OF EAGLES
YEAR OF THE TIGER
DRINK WITH THE DEVIL
NIGHT JUDGEMENT AT SINOS
ANGEL OF DEATH
SHEBA
ON DANGEROUS GROUND
THUNDER POINT
EYE OF THE STORM (*also published as*
MIDNIGHT MAN)
THE EAGLE HAS FLOWN
COLD HARBOUR
MEMORIES OF A DANCE-HALL ROMEO
A SEASON IN HELL
NIGHT OF THE FOX
CONFESSIONAL
EXOCET
TOUCH THE DEVIL
LUCIANO'S LUCK
SOLO
DAY OF JUDGMENT
STORM WARNING
THE LAST PLACE GOD MADE
A PRAYER FOR THE DYING
THE EAGLE HAS LANDED
THE RUN TO MORNING
DILLINGER
TO CATCH A KING
THE VALHALLA EXCHANGE

JACK HIGGINS

YEAR OF THE TIGER

BERKLEY BOOKS, NEW YORK

This is a work of fiction. Names, characters, places, and incidents are either the product of the author's imagination or are used fictitiously, and any resemblance to actual persons, living or dead, business establishments, events, or locales is entirely coincidental.

Elements from this novel are taken from a novel of the same title published in 1963 under the pseudonym Martin Fallon by Abelard-Schuman, London.

YEAR OF THE TIGER

A Berkley Book / pubished by arrangement with Higgins Associates Limited

PRINTING HISTORY
Berkley edition / October 1996

The Penguin Putnam Inc. World Wide Web site address is http://www.penguinputnam.com

ISBN: 0-425-15517-X

BERKLEY®
Berkley Books are published by The Berkley Publishing Group, a division of Penguin Putnam Inc., 375 Hudson Street, New York, New York 10014.
BERKLEY and the "B" design are trademarks belonging to Penguin Putnam Inc.

PRINTED IN THE UNITED STATES OF AMERICA

10   9   8   7

In March 1959, after the failure of the revolt by the Tibetan people against their Chinese masters, the Dalai Lama, with the help of the CIA and British intelligence sources, escaped to India. A remarkable affair, and yet three years later the British masterminded an even more remarkable coup. It went something like this . . .

LONDON

....

1995

1

They were closer now; he could hear the savage barking of the dogs, the voices of his pursuers calling to each other, firing at random as he ran headlong through the trees. There was a chance, although not much of a one, if he could reach the river and cross to the other side. Another country and home free. He slipped and fell, rolling over and over as the ground sloped. As he got to his feet there was an enormous clap of thunder, the skies opened and rain fell in a great curtain, blanketing everything. No scent for the dogs now and he started to run again, laughing wildly, aware of the sound of the river, very close now, knowing that he'd won again this damned game he'd been playing for so long. He burst out of the trees and found himself on a bluff, the river swollen and angry below him, mist shrouding the other side. It was at this moment that another volley of rifle shots rang out. A solid hammerlike blow on his left shoulder punched him forward over the edge of the bluff into the swirling waters. He seemed to go down forever, then started to kick desperately, trying for the surface, a surface that wasn't there. He was choking now, at the final end of things and still fighting and suddenly, he broke through and took a great lungful of air.

Paul Chavasse came awake with a start. The room was in darkness. He was sprawled in one of the two great armchairs which stood on either side of the fireplace and the fire was low, the only light in the room on a dark November evening. The file from the Bureau which he'd been reading was on the floor at his feet. He must have dozed and then the dream. Strange, he hadn't had that one in years, but it was real enough, and his hand instinctively touched his left shoulder where the old scar was still plain to see. *A long time ago*.

The clock on the mantelshelf chimed six times and he got to his feet and reached to turn on the lamp on the table beside him. He hesitated, remembering, and moved to the windows, where the curtains were still open. He peered out into St. Martin's Square.

It was as quiet as usual, the gardens and trees

in the centre touched by fog. There was a light on at the windows of the church opposite, the usual number of parked cars. Then there was a movement in the shadows by the garden railings opposite the house and the woman was there again. Old-fashioned trilby hat, what looked like a Burberry trench coat and a skirt beneath, reaching to the ankles. She stood there in the light of a lamp, looking across at the house, then slipped back into the shadows, an elusive figure.

Chavasse drew the curtains, switched on the lights and picked up the phone. He called through to the basement flat where Earl Jackson, his official driver from the Ministry of Defence, lived with his wife, Lucy, who acted as cook and housekeeper.

Jackson's voice had a hard Cockney edge to it. "What can I do for you, Sir Paul?"

Chavasse winced. He still couldn't get used to the title, which was hardly surprising, for he had only been knighted by the Queen a week previously.

"Listen, Earl, there's a strange woman lurking around in the shadows opposite. Wears an old trilby hat, Burberry, skirt down to the ankles. Could be a bag lady, but it's the third night running that I've seen her. Somehow I get a funny feeling."

"That's why you're still here," Jackson said. "I'll check her out."

"Take it easy," Chavasse told him. "Send Lucy

to the corner shop and she can have a look on the way. Less obvious."

"Leave it with me," Jackson said. "Are we going out?"

"Well, I need to eat. Let's make it The Garrick. I'll be ready at seven."

He shaved first, an old habit, showered afterwards, then towelled himself vigorously. He paused to touch the scar of the bullet wound on the left shoulder, then ran his finger across a similar scar on his chest on the right side with the six-inch line below it where a very dangerous young woman had tried to gut him with a knife more years ago than he cared to remember.

He slipped the towel around his waist and combed his hair, white at the temples now but still dark, though not as dark as the eyes in a handsome, rather aristocratic face. The high cheekbones were a legacy of his Breton father, the slightly world-weary look of a man who had seen too much of the dark side of life.

"Still, not bad for sixty-five, old stick," he said softly. "Only what comes now? D day tomorrow!"

It was his private and not very funny joke, for the D stood for disposal and on the following day he was retiring from the Bureau, that most elusive of all sections of the British Secret Intelligence Service. Forty years: twenty as a field agent, another twenty as Chief after his old boss had died, not that it had turned out to be the usual kind of desk job—not with the Irish troubles.

So now it was all over, he told himself as he dressed quickly in a soft white shirt and an easy-fitting dark blue Armani suit. No more passion, no more action by night, he thought as he knotted his tie. And no woman in his life to fall back on, although there had always been plenty available. The trouble was that the only one he had truly loved had died far too early and far too brutally. Even the revenge he had exacted had failed to take away the bitter taste. Yes, there had been women in his life, but never another he had wanted to marry.

He went into the drawing room and picked up the phone. "I'm on my way, Earl."

"I'll be ready, Sir Paul."

Chavasse pulled on a navy blue raincoat, switched off the light and went downstairs.

Earl Jackson was black, a fact which had given him no trouble at all with the more racist elements in the British army, where he had served in both 1 Para and the SAS, mainly because he was six feet four in height and still a trim fifteen stone in spite of being forty-four years of age. He'd earned a Distinguished Conduct Metal in the Falklands and he and his wife, Lucy, had been with Chavasse for ten years now.

It had started to rain and when Chavasse

opened the front door he found Jackson waiting with a raised umbrella, very smart in grey uniform and peaked cap. As they went down the steps to the Jaguar, Chavasse glanced across at the garden. There was a slight movement in the shadows.

"Still there?"

"He certainly is," Jackson told him, and opened the passenger door at the front, for Chavasse always sat with him.

"You mean it's a man?" Chavasse said as he got in.

Jackson shut the door, put the umbrella down and slid behind the wheel. "But no ordinary man." He started the engine. "Lucy says he's sort of Chinese."

Jackson drove away and Chavasse said, "What does she mean by 'sort of'?"

"She says there's something different about him. Not really like any Chinese she knows and quite different from those Thais and Koreans you see in their restaurants."

Chavasse nodded. "And the skirt?"

"She just got a glimpse while he was under the lamp. She said it seemed like some sort of robe and as far as she could make out in the bad light it was a kind of yellow colour."

Chavasse frowned. "Curiouser and curiouser."

"You want me to do something about it, Sir Paul?"

"Not for the moment," Chavasse told him,

"and stop calling me Sir Paul. We've been to
gether too long."

"I'll do my best." Earl Jackson smiled. "But
you'll be wasting your time with Lucy. She just
loves it," and he turned out onto the main road
and picked up speed.

The porter at The Garrick, that most exclusive
of London clubs, greeted him with a smile and
took his coat.

"Nice to see you, Sir Paul." He came out with
the title as if he'd been doing it all his life.

Chavasse gave up and mounted the majestic
staircase, with its stunning collection of oil paint-
ings, and went into the bar. A couple of ageing
gentlemen sat in the corner talking quietly, but
otherwise the place was empty.

"Good evening, Sir Paul," the barman said.
There it was again. "Your usual?"

"Why not?"

Chavasse went and sat in a corner, took out his
old silver case and lit a cigarette while the barman
brought a bottle of Bollinger RD Champagne,
opened it and poured. Chavasse tried it, nodded
his satisfaction and the barman topped up the
glass and retreated.

Chavasse toasted himself. "Well, here's to you,
old stick," he murmured. "But what comes next,
that's the thing."

He emptied the glass rather quickly, refilled it
and sat back. At that moment a young man en-

tered, paused, glancing around, then approached him.

"Sir Paul Chavasse? Terry Williams of the prime minister's office."

"You must be new," Chavasse said. "I don't think we've met."

"Very new, sir. We were trying to get hold of you and your housekeeper told us you would be here."

"Sounds urgent," Chavasse said.

"The prime minister wanted a word, that's the thing."

Chavasse frowned. "Do you know what it's about?"

"I'm afraid not." Williams smiled cheerfully. "But I'm sure he'll tell you himself. He's on the way up."

A moment later John Major, the British prime minister, entered the bar.

His personal detective was behind him and waited by the entrance. The prime minister was in evening dress and smiled as he came forward and held out his hand.

"Good to see you, Paul."

Williams withdrew discreetly and Chavasse said, "Thank God you didn't say Sir Paul. I'm damned if I can get used to it."

John Major sat down. "You got used to being called the Chief for the past twenty years."

"Yes, well that was carrying on a Bureau

tradition set up by my predecessor," Chavasse told him. "Can I offer you a glass of champagne?"

"No thanks. The reason for my rather glamourous appearance is that I'm on my way to a fund-raising affair at the Dorchester and they'll try and thrust enough glasses of champagne on to me there."

Chavasse raised his glass and toasted him. "Congratulations on your leadership victory, Prime Minister."

"Yes, I'm still here," Major said. "Both of us are."

"Not me," Chavasse reminded him. "Last day tomorrow."

"Yes, well that's what I wanted to speak to you about. How long have you been with the Bureau, Paul?" He smiled. "Don't answer, I've been through your record. Twenty years as a field agent, shot three times, knifed twice. You've had as many injuries as a National Hunt jockey."

Chavasse smiled. "Just about."

"Then twenty as Chief and thanks to the Irish situation, leading just as hazardous a life as when you were a field agent." The prime minister shook his head. "I don't think we can let all that experience go."

"But my knighthood," Chavasse said, "the ritual pat on the head on the way out. I must remind you, Prime Minister, that I'm sixty-five years of age."

"Nonsense," John Major told him. "Sixty-five going on fifty." He leaned forward. "All this trouble in what used to be Yugoslavia and Ireland is not proving as easy as we'd hoped." He shook his head. "No, Paul, we need you. I need you. Frankly, I haven't even considered a successor."

At that moment Williams came forward. "Sorry, Prime Minister, but I must remind you of the time."

John Major nodded and stood. Chavasse did the same. "I don't know what to say."

"Think about it and let me know." He shook Chavasse by the hand. "Must go. Let me hear from you," and he turned and walked out, followed by his detective and Williams.

And think about it Chavasse did as he sat at the long table in the dining room and had a cold lobster salad, washing it down with the rest of the champagne. It was crazy. All those years. A miracle that he'd survived and just when he was out, they wanted him back in.

He had two cups of coffee then went downstairs, recovered his raincoat and went down the steps to the street. The Jaguar was parked nearby and Jackson was out in a second and had the door open.

"Nice meal?" he asked.

"I can't remember."

Jackson got behind the wheel and started up. "You all right?"

Chavasse said, "What would you say if I told you the prime minister wants me to stay on?"

"Good God!" Jackson said, and swerved slightly.

"Exactly."

"Will you?"

"I don't know, Earl, I really don't," and Chavasse lit a cigarette and leaned back.

As they reached the turning into St. Martin's Square, Chavasse said, "Stop here. I'll walk the rest of the way. Time I took a look for myself."

"You sure you'll be all right?" Jackson asked.

"Of course. Give me the umbrella."

Chavasse got out, put up the umbrella against the relentless rain, walked along the wet pavement until he came to the next turning, which brought him into the Square on the opposite side from his house. He paused. There was a touch of fog in the rain and he seemed to sense voices and laughter. He crossed to the entrance to the garden in the centre of the Square.

The voices were clearer now, the laughter callous and brutal. He hurried forward and saw the mystery man clear in the light of a street lamp, being manhandled by three youths. They were typical of a type to be found in any city in the world, vicious animals in bomber jackets and jeans.

One of them wore a baseball cap and seemed to be the leader. He swatted the mystery man across the side of the head and the trilby hat went flying, revealing a shaven skull.

"Christ, what have we got here?" the youth in the baseball cap demanded. "A bloody Chink. Hold him while I give him a slapping."

Chavasse, seeing the man's face clear in the light of the street lamp, knew what he was. *Tibetan*. The other two lads grabbed the man by the arms and the one in the baseball cap raised a fist.

Chavasse didn't say a word, simply stamped hard against the back of the lad's left knee, sending him sprawling. The youth lay there for a moment, glowering up.

"Let's call it a night," Chavasse said, putting down his umbrella.

The other two released the Tibetan and rushed in. Chavasse rammed the end of the umbrella hard into the groin of one and turned sideways, then stamped on the kneecap of the second, sending him down with a cry of agony.

He heard a click behind and the Tibetan called, "Watch out!"

As Chavasse turned, the one in the baseball cap was on his feet, a switchblade in one hand, murder in his eyes. Suddenly, Earl Jackson seemed to materialise from the gloom like some dark shadow.

"Can anyone join in?" he enquired.

The youth turned and slashed at him. Jackson caught the wrist with effortless ease, then twisted hard. The youth dropped the knife and cried out in pain as something snapped.

Jackson picked up the knife, stepped on the blade and dropped it down the gutter drain. The other two were on their feet, but in poor condition. Baseball cap was sobbing in pain.

"Nigger bastard," he snarled.

"That's right, boy, and don't you forget it. I'm your worst nightmare. Now go."

They limped away together, disappearing into the night, and Chavasse said, "Good man, Earl. My thanks."

"Getting too old for this kind of game," Jackson said. "And so are you. Think about that."

The Tibetan stood there holding his trilby, rain falling on the shaven head, the yellowing saffron robes beneath the raincoat indicating one thing only: that this was a Buddhist monk. He looked about thirty-five, with a calm and placid face.

"A violent world on occasion, Sir Paul."

"Well you're up to date at least," Chavasse told him. "Why have you been hanging around for the last three days?"

"I wished to see you."

"Then why not knock on the door?"

"I feared I might be turned away without the opportunity of seeing you. I am Tibetan."

"I can tell that."

"I know that I seem strange to many people. My appearance alarms some." He shrugged. "I thought it simpler to wait in the hope of seeing you in the street."

"Where you end up at the mercy of animals like those."

The Tibetan shrugged. "They are young, they are foolish, they are not responsible. The fox kills the chicken. It is his nature. Should I then kill the fox?"

"I sure as hell would if it was my chicken," Earl Jackson said.

"But that would make me no follower of Lord Buddha." He turned to Chavasse. "As you may be able to tell I am a Buddhist monk. My name is Lama Moro. I am a monk in the Tibetan temple at Glen Aristoun in Scotland."

"Christ said that if a man slaps you across the check turn the other one, but he only told us to do it once," Chavasse said. Jackson laughed out loud. Chavasse carried on. "Have you eaten?"

"A little rice this morning."

Chavasse turned to Jackson. "Earl, take him to the kitchen. Let him discuss his diet with Lucy. Tell her to feed him. Then bring him up to me."

"You are a kind man, Sir Paul," Lama Moro said.

"No, just a wet one," Chavasse told him. "So let's get in out of the rain," and he led the way across the road.

An hour later there was a knock at the drawing room door and in came Lucy, the apple of

Jackson's eye, a face on her like that of some ancient Egyptian princess, her hair tied in a velvet bow, neat in a black dress and apron.

"I've got him for you, Sir Paul. Lucky I had plenty of rice and vegetables in. He's a nice man. I like him." She stood back and Moro entered in his saffron robes. "I've got his raincoat and hat in the cloakroom," she added, and left.

A glass in his hand, Chavasse was sitting in one of the armchairs beside the fire, which burned brightly.

"Come and sit down."

"You are too kind." Moro sat in the chair opposite him.

"I won't offer you one of these." Chavasse raised the glass. "It's Bushmills Irish whiskey, the oldest in the world, some say, and invented by monks."

"How enterprising."

"You're a long way from home," Chavasse said.

"Not really. I left Tibet with other refugees when I was fifteen years of age. That was in 1975."

"I see. And since then?"

"Three years with the Dalai Lama in India, then he arranged for me to go to Cambridge to your old college—Trinity. You were also at the Sorbonne. I too have studied there, but Harvard eluded me."

"You certainly know a great deal about me," Chavasse told him.

17

"Oh, yes," Moro said calmly. "Your father was French."

"Breton," Chavasse said. "There is a difference."

"Of course. Your mother was English. You had a unique gift for languages, which explains your studies at three of the world's greatest universities. A Ph.D. at twenty-one, you returned to Cambridge to your own college, where they made you a Fellow at twenty-three. So there you were, at an exceptionally young age, set on an academic career at a great university."

"And then?" Chavasse enquired.

"You had a colleague at Trinity whose daughter was married to a Czech. When he died, she wanted to return to England with her children. The Communists refused to let her go and the British Foreign Office wouldn't help." Moro shrugged. "You went in on your own initiative and got them out, sustaining a slight wound from a border guard's rifle."

"Ah, the foolishness of youth," Chavasse said.

"Safely back at Cambridge, you were visited by Sir Ian Moncrieff, known only as the Chief in intelligence circles, the man who controlled the Bureau, the most secret of all British intelligence units."

"Where in the hell did you get all this from?" Chavasse demanded.

"Sources of my own," Moro told him. "Twenty years in the field for the Bureau and twenty years as Chief after Moncrieff's death. A remarkable record."

"The only thing remarkable about it is that I'm still here," Chavasse said. "Now who exactly are you?"

"As I told you, I'm from the Tibetan temple at Glen Aristoun in Scotland."

"I've heard of it," Chavasse told him. "A Buddhist community."

"I live and work there. I am the librarian. I have been collating information on the escape of the Dalai Lama from Tibet in March 1959."

A great light dawned. "Oh, I see now," Chavasse said. "You've found out that I was there. That I was one of those who got him out."

"Yes, I know all about that, Sir Paul, heard of those adventures from the Dalai Lama's own lips. No, it is what comes after that interests me."

"And what would that be?" Chavasse asked warily.

"In 1962, exactly three years after you helped the Dalai Lama to escape, you returned to Tibet to the town of Changu to effect the escape of Dr. Karl Hoffner, who'd worked as a medical missionary in the area for years."

"Karl Hoffner?" Chavasse said.

"One of the greatest mathematicians of the century," Moro said. "As great as Einstein." He was almost impatient now. "Come, Sir Paul, I know from sound sources that you undertook the mission, and yet there is no record of Hoffner other than his time in Tibet. Did he die there? What happened?"

"Why do you wish to know?"

"For the record. The history of my country's troubled times under Chinese rule. Please, Sir Paul, is there any reason for secrecy after thirty-four years?"

"No, I suppose not." Chavasse poured another whiskey. "All right. Strictly off the record, of course. Flight of fancy when you put it on the page."

"I agree. You can trust me."

Chavasse sipped a little Bushmills. "So, where to begin?"

But where did anything begin? A long time ago, he told himself. A hell of a long time ago.

TIBET

....

1959

2

Chavasse wore a sheepskin *shuba* wrapped closely around him, sheepskin boots and a hat of some indeterminate fur, flaps down over his ears. He cradled a British Lee Enfield rifle in one arm and allowed the hardy mountain pony to find its own way. He thought he heard a plane at one point, but could not be sure as the sound faded rapidly.

The Land of Snows the Tibetans called this part of the border area, and it was well named, a living nightmare of a place with passes through the mountains as high as twenty thousand feet. It was not uncommon for mules in the caravans in the old days to die of asthma and for their masters to get pulmonary edema as their lungs filled with water.

An ironic way to die, Chavasse thought, to

drown while standing up. Of course, it didn't matter these days. There were no more caravans to India, by Chinese decree.

It started to snow again lightly and he paused to check the ground ahead. The sky being blanketed by low swollen clouds, there was no snow glare. He had spent the previous night in a herdsman's cave, sheltering from a sudden blizzard, and had started again at first light. Now, the pass between the peaks emptied onto a final slope that ran down towards the Indian border. In fact, in the far distance there was a flicker of colour, obviously a flag, and Chavasse urged his pony forward.

24

The border post was quite simple. A large stone hut, no barbed wire, no defence system. Half a dozen Indian soldiers stood outside wearing white winter combat uniforms, the hoods pulled up over their turbans. There was a jeep painted in white camouflage, and the young man leaning against it smoking a cigarette came forward and looked up at Chavasse.

"Mr. Chavasse? I am Lieutenant Piroo. We heard over the radio from Tibetan freedom fighters that you were coming." He smiled. "I'm surprised that there are any left, if the reports we get of Chinese reaction are true."

Chavasse heaved himself out of the saddle and a soldier led the pony away. "Oh, they're true all right. They're killing people by the thousands, wiping out whole villages." Piroo gave him a cigarette and lit it for him and Chavasse continued. "No, I'm afraid this time they intend to wipe out Tibetan resistance once and for all."

"Which is why the Dalai Lama has fled?"

"Yes, he hopes to continue the struggle from India. Do you think Prime Minister Nehru will accept him?"

"Oh, yes, that has been made quite clear. But come, Mr. Chavasse, my boss is waiting to see you at Gela. That's about ten miles from here." He smiled. "And only sixteen thousand feet."

Chavasse got into the jeep and Piroo slipped behind the wheel. "And who might your boss be?"

"Colonel Ram Singh. Very correct and old school. Even went to Sandhurst." Piroo, in spite of the jeep sliding from side to side on the rough track, found another cigarette and lit it one-handed. "I thought the CIA were to do great things? Help the rebels and so on?"

"They dropped in a certain amount of arms," Chavasse told him. "Mostly British, because they didn't want the Chinese to make an American connection. Other than that, they haven't done much."

"But you have, Mr. Chavasse. British intelligence still functions, it would seem."

"So they tell me."

"I understand you were told by the Indian

government not to cross the border, but went anyway?"

"That's true."

"And Major Hamid went with you?"

"Also true."

Piroo shook his head. "Crazy Pathan. They'll court-martial him for this."

"No they won't. He's behind me right now with the Dalai Lama. I only came ahead to confirm their arrival time. Hamid will be an instant hero to every Indian on this continent."

"Perhaps not, my friend."

"And what do you mean by that?" Chavasse demanded.

"Oh, that's for my boss to tell you."

Chavasse sat there, frowning, and they came over a rise and saw a number of Nissen huts below beside an airstrip. The aircraft parked at one end had twin engines and was painted white.

"A Navajo," Chavasse said. "What's that doing here?"

"A quick link with the lowlands. Supplies, communications. The Airstair door means we can get stretchers in."

"And why the white strip?"

"So that if I stray over the border it will make it more difficult for the Chinese to shoot me down." Piroo smiled. "Oh, yes, Mr. Chavasse. I am the pilot. Indian air force, not army," and he drove down the track.

* * *

It was warm in the Nissen hut as the four officers and Chavasse leaned over the map on the table. Colonel Ram Singh was small and fierce with a thin moustache, the medal ribbons on his shirt making a fine show.

"Not good, Mr. Chavasse, not good. I can tell you unofficially that Prime Minister Nehru and the Indian government are prepared to receive the Dalai Lama. Piroo here was to fly him out as soon as he arrived."

"Which isn't likely now, I'm afraid," Piroo said. "I made an overflight—quite illegally, of course." His finger touched the map. "Here is the Dalai Lama's column. I'd estimate by now about fifteen miles to go." He indicated again. "And here, twenty-five miles behind them, a Chinese column coming up fast—jeeps, not horses. Certain to catch them before the border."

Chavasse examined the map carefully. "When did you see all this?"

"An hour ago. Not much more."

Chavasse nodded. "I came that way myself. The terrain is terrible. Even a jeep is lucky to cover ten miles in an hour. Rough ground and boulders everywhere."

"So?" Ram Singh said.

"That means the Chinese are still on the other side of the Cholo Gorge. Hundreds of feet deep. There's an old wooden bridge there. It's the only way across. Destroy that and they've had it. The Dalai Lama will be home free."

"An attractive idea, Mr. Chavasse, but if you are suggesting that Lieutenant Piroo should somehow bomb their bridge, I must say no. Chinese territory, that is what they claim, and we are not at war with China."

"Well I am." Chavasse turned to Piroo. "You carry parachutes on that thing?"

"Of course."

Chavasse said to Ram Singh, "Meet me halfway, Colonel. You've already allowed Piroo to fly over there. Let him volunteer again. You find me some explosives. On the way in we drop a message to the Dalai Lama's column to alert Hamid as to what's going on, then I'll parachute in at the bridge and blow it up."

"But what happens after?" Piroo demanded. "You'll be all alone out there on foot."

"Hopefully Hamid will ride back for me."

There was a long silence as all the officers exchanged glances. The colonel looked down at the map, drumming his fingers on it. He glanced up.

"You would do this, Lieutenant?" he asked Piroo.

"My pleasure, Colonel."

"Madness," Ram Singh said. "Total madness." Suddenly he smiled. "We'd better get cracking, Mr. Chavasse. Not much time."

*   *   *

Ram Singh said, "A very simple explosive, Mr. Chavasse." He opened an army haversack and produced one of several dark green blocks. "We get it from the French army."

"Plastique," Chavasse said.

"Totally harmless until used in conjunction with one of these timer pencils." Ram Singh held a few up. "Five-minute fuses, but the two with yellow ends are two minutes."

The haversack was put on Chavasse's back, then he pushed his arms through the straps. One of the officers helped him into a parachute, another gave him a Sten gun with two magazines taped together, which he draped across his chest.

Ram Singh picked up a weighted signal can with a great scarlet streamer attached to it. "The message for Major Hamid. It tells him exactly what you intend." Ram Singh put a hand on Chavasse's shoulder. "I hope he finds it possible to . . . how shall I put it . . . to retrieve you, my friend."

"He's a Pathan," Chavasse said simply. "You know what they're like. He'd walk into the jaws of hell just to have a look." He smiled. "I'd better get moving."

Ram Singh pulled on a parka and led the way out. It was snowing a little, loose flakes on the wind and very cold. They crossed to the Navajo, where Piroo already had the engines warming up. Chavasse paused at the bottom of the Airstair door and Ram Singh shook hands and saluted.

"As God wills, my friend."

Chavasse smiled, went up the steps and pushed the door shut. Piroo glanced over his shoulder and boosted power, then they roared along the airstrip and lifted off.

In spite of the layers of clothing he wore, Chavasse was cold—very cold—and he found breathing difficult. He looked out of the window to a landscape as barren as the moon, snow-covered peaks on either side. Now and then they dropped sickeningly in an air pocket, and they were constantly buffeted by strong winds.

Piroo glanced over his shoulder and shouted above the roar of the engines.

"I'll curve round to the gorge first. Let's make sure the Chinese are still on the other side before we communicate with Hamid."

"Fine," Chavasse told him.

They entered a low cloud which enveloped them for five minutes. Then they came out on the other side and there was the gorge below, the bridge in clear view. Even clearer was the Chinese column perhaps a quarter of a mile on the other side, racing towards the bridge very fast over what was at that point a flat plain.

"No time to hang around. They'll be at the bridge in ten minutes," Chavasse shouted. "I'm on my way. Take me down to five hundred."

Piroo dropped the nose, and the Navajo went down and levelled out. Chavasse moved awkwardly because of the bulk of his equipment and released the Airstair door. There was a great rush of air. He waited until they were as close to the bridge as possible, then tumbled out headfirst.

Hamid dismounted and waited while one of the Tibetan freedom fighters galloped to where the signal can lay on the snow, the scarlet streamer plain. The man leaned down from the saddle, picked up the can and galloped back.

Hamid was a typical Pathan, a large man, very tall, dark-skinned and with a proud look to his bearded face. Behind him the column had stopped as everyone waited. The horsemen arrived and handed over the can. Hamid opened it and took out the message and read it. He swore softly.

From behind, a voice called, "What is it, Major Hamid?"

The Dalai Lama, covered by sheepskins, lay on a kind of trailer pulled by a horse, for he was too ill to ride.

"It's from Chavasse."

"So he got through?"

"Unfortunately there's a Chinese column very close to us on the other side of the Cholo Gorge. It would seem Chavasse has dropped in by parachute in an effort to blow the bridge. I must go to his aid."

"I understand," the Dalai Lama said.

31

"Good. I'll take two of the escorts with me. The rest of you must press on with all possible speed."

He rode across to one of the carts and picked up a Bren gun and two magazines, which he stuffed into his saddlebag, then he gave a quick order to two of the Tibetans and galloped away. A few moments later, leading a spare horse, they went after him.

Chavasse hit the ground heavily perhaps a hundred yards from the bridge. He lay there for a moment, winded, then stood up and struggled out of his parachute harness. There was still no sign of the Chinese and he unslung the Sten gun and ran along the uneven track between outcrops of rock.

It was stupid, of course, such exertion of that altitude, and by the time he reached the bridge he was gasping for air, his breath like white smoke. He started across and it swayed gently. He got to the centre, took off the haversack and selected a block of plastique, inserted a five-minute timer, lay down and reached over the edge and wedged the explosive into a space between the ends of two struts. He activated the timer and stood up, and at that moment a Chinese jeep appeared on top of the rise on the other side.

Its machine gun opened up at once. Chavasse ran, the Sten gun in one hand, the haversack in the other. He reached the end of the bridge, ducked behind one of the supporting posts, found another block of plastique, inserted a yellow two-minute fuse and activated it.

The jeep kept firing, bullets clipping wood from the post. He laid the plastique block down and returned fire with his Sten, and a lucky shot knocked one soldier out. The jeep, halfway across the bridge, paused, with another just behind it, and on the ridge above the rest of the column arrived.

"Just stay there," Chavasse prayed, and tossed the block of plastique out onto the bridge.

To his horror, it actually bounced over the edge, where it exploded in space. Firing relentlessly, the jeep started forward, followed by the other, and the column moved down on the other side.

Chavasse ran up amongst the rocks, head down, glancing back to see the two jeeps reach firm ground. At that moment and just as the convoy started across, there was a huge explosion. The centre of the bridge twisted up into the air, lengths of timber flying everywhere. The two lead jeeps in the convoy on the other side went with it.

As the reverberations died away there were cries of rage from the Chinese in the two jeeps that had got across, three soldiers in one and four in the other. They fired their light machine guns into the rocks below the escarpment and Chavasse cowered down and opened his haversack. There was one block of plastique left. He inserted the remaining two-minute pencil and started to count, the Sten gun ready in his other hand.

He fired it in short sharp bursts with his left hand, still counting, and the soldiers raked the rocks with machine-gun fire so fierce that he had to keep his head down and hurl the block of plastique blindly. This time his luck was good, for it landed in the jeep containing four soldiers and exploded a second later, with devastating effect.

He glanced over a rock and saw only carnage. The four soldiers had been killed outright and the other jeep tilted on one side, its three occupants having been thrown from it. As Chavasse watched, they got to their feet, coughing in the acrid smoke, and picked up their weapons. He stood and opened fire with the Sten, three bullets kicking up dirt beside them. Then the magazine simply emptied itself. He threw it down, turned and ran for his life as the three Chinese cried out and came after him.

Bullets ploughed into the ground beside him, kicking up snow as he struggled up the slope, and then a cheerful voice cried, "Lie down, Paul, for God's sake."

Hamid appeared on the ridge above, holding the Bren light machine gun in both hands. He swept it from side to side, cutting down the three

Chinese in a second. As the echoes died away, he looked at the ruins of the bridge.

"Now that's what I call close."

"You could say that." Chavasse scrambled up the slope and saw the two Tibetans below holding Hamid's horse and the spare. "How thoughtful—you've brought one for me. Prime Minister Nehru and the Indian government are prepared to receive the Dalai Lama. The Indian air force plane that just dropped me in will be waiting on the airstrip at Gela. We'll all be in Delhi before you know it."

"Excellent," Hamid said. "So can we kindly get the hell out of here?"

The British embassy in Delhi was ablaze with light, crystal chandeliers glittering, the fans in the ceiling stirring the warm air, the French windows open to the gardens.

The ballroom was packed with people, anyone who counted in Delhi, the great and the good, not only the British ambassador, but Prime Minister Nehru, all there to honour the Dalai Lama, who sat in a chair by the main entrance, greeting the well-wishers who passed him in line.

Chavasse, in a white linen suit, black shirt and pale lemon tie, stood watching. Hamid was at his side, resplendent in turban and khaki uniform, his medal ribbons, particularly the Military Cross from the British, making a brave show.

"Look at them," Chavasse said. "All they want

to do is to be able to boast that they shook his hand. They'd ask for his autograph if they dared."

"The way of the world, Paul," the Pathan told him.

There was a Chinese in the line, a small man with horn-rimmed glasses, an eager smile on his face. Chavasse stiffened.

"Who's that?"

The young lieutenant behind them said, "His name is Chung. He's a doctor. Runs a clinic for the poor. He's Chinese Nationalist from Formosa. Came here six months ago."

Dr. Chung took the Dalai Lama's hand. "Chung—Formosa, Holiness," they heard him say. "Such an honour."

The Dalai Lama murmured a response, and Chung moved away and took a glass from a tray held by one of the many turbanned waiters.

The Dalai Lama beckoned the young lieutenant, and said to him, "Enough for the moment. I think I'll have a turn in the garden. I could do with some fresh air." He smiled at Chavasse and Hamid. "I'll see you again in a little while, gentlemen."

Escorted by the lieutenant, he made his way through the crowd, nodding and smiling to people as he passed, then went out through one of the French windows. The lieutenant returned.

"He seems tired. I'll just go and tell them at

the door to warn new guests that he's not available for presentation."

He walked away and Hamid said, "When do you return to London?"

Chavasse lit a cigarette. "Not sure. I'm waiting for orders from my boss."

"Ah, the Chief, the famous Sir Ian Moncrieff."

"You're not supposed to know that," Chavasse said.

"No, you're certainly not," a familiar voice said.

Chavasse swung round in astonishment and found Moncrieff standing there. He wore a crumpled sand-coloured linen suit and a Guards tie, and his grey hair was swept back.

"Where on earth did you spring from?" Chavasse demanded.

"The flight from London that got in two hours ago. Magnificent job, Paul. Thought I'd join in the festivities." He turned to the Pathan. "You'll be Hamid?"

They shook hands. "A pleasure, Sir Ian."

Moncrieff took a glass from the tray of a passing waiter and Chavasse said, "Well, they're all here, as you can see."

Moncrieff drank some of the wine. "Including the opposition."

"What do you mean?" Hamid asked.

"Our Chinese friend over there." Moncrieff indicated Chung, who was working his way through the crowd towards the French windows.

"Chinese Nationalist from Formosa," Chavasse said. "Runs a clinic for the poor downtown."

"Well, if that's what Indian intelligence believe they're singularly ill-informed. I saw his picture in a file at the Chinese Section of SIS in London only last month. He's a Communist agent. Where's the Dalai Lama, by the way?"

"In the garden," Hamid told him.

At that moment Chung went out through one of the open French windows. "Come on," Chavasse said to Hamid, and pushed his way quickly through the crowd. The garden was very beautiful—flowers everywhere, the scent of magnolias heavy on the night air, palm trees swaying in a light breeze. The spray from a large fountain in the centre of the garden lifted into the night and the Dalai Lama followed a path towards it, alone with his thoughts. He paused as Dr. Chung stepped from the bushes.

"Holiness, forgive me, but your time has come."

He held an automatic pistol in one hand, a silencer on the end. The Dalai Lama took it in and smiled serenely.

"I forgive you, my son. Death comes to all men."

Hamid, running fast, Chavasse at his back, was on Chung in an instant, one arm around his neck, a hand reaching for the right wrist, depressing the weapon towards the ground. It fired once, a dull thud, and Chung, struggling desperately, managed to turn. For a moment they were breast to breast, the tall Pathan and the small Chinese. After another dull thud, Chung went rigid and slumped to the ground. For a moment he lay there kicking, then he went very still.

Chavasse went down on one knee and examined him as Moncrieff arrived on the run. Chavasse stood up, the gun in his hand.

"Is he dead?" the Dalai Lama asked.

"Yes," Chavasse told him.

"May his soul be at peace."

"I'd suggest you come with me, sir," Moncrieff said. "The fewer people who know about this the better. In fact it never happened, did it, Major?"

"I'll handle it, sir," Hamid said. "Utmost discretion. I'll get the head of security."

Moncrieff took the Dalai Lama away. Hamid said, "Pity the poor sod decided to shoot himself here, and we'll never know why, will we? As good a story as any. You stay here, Paul. You'll make a fine witness, and so will I." He shook his head. "Peking has a long arm."

The Pathan hurried away and Chavasse lit a cigarette and went and sat on a bench by the fountain and waited.

LONDON
1962

3

Chavasse stood in the entrance of the Caravel Club on Great Portland Street and looked gloomily out into the driving rain. He had conducted a wary love affair with London for several years, but four o'clock on a wet November morning was enough to strain any relationship, he told himself as he stepped out onto the pavement.

There was a nasty taste in his mouth from too many cigarettes, and the thought of the 115 pounds which had passed across the green baize tables of the Caravel didn't help matters.

He'd been hanging around town for too long, that was the trouble. It was now over two months since he'd returned from his vacation after the Caspar Schultz affair, and the Chief had kept him sitting behind a desk at headquarters dealing with paperwork that any reasonably competent general-grade clerk could have handled.

He was still considering the situation and wondering what to do about it when he turned the corner onto Baker Street, looked up casually and noticed the light in his apartment.

He crossed the street quickly and went through the swing doors. The foyer was deserted and the night porter wasn't behind his desk. Chavasse stood there thinking about it for a moment, a slight frown on his face. He finally decided against using the lift and went up the stairs quickly to the third floor.

The corridor was wrapped in quiet. He paused outside the door to his apartment for a moment, listening, and then moved round the corner to the service entrance and took out his key.

The plump woman who sat on the edge of the kitchen table reading a magazine as she waited for the coffeepot to boil was attractive in spite of her dark, rather severe spectacles.

Chavasse closed the door gently, tiptoed across the room and kissed her on the nape of the neck. "I must say this is a funny time to call, but I'm more than willing," he said with a grin.

Jean Frazer, the Chief's secretary, turned and looked at him calmly. "Don't flatter yourself, and where the hell have you been? I've had scouts out all over Soho and the West End since eight o'clock last night."

A cold finger of excitement moved inside him. "Something big turned up."

She nodded. "You're telling me. You'd better go in. The Chief's been here since midnight hoping you'd turn up."

"How about some coffee?"

"I'll bring it in when it's ready." She wrinkled her nose. "You've been drinking again, haven't you?"

"What a hell of a wife you'd make, sweetheart," he told her with a tired grin, and went through into the living room.

Two men were sitting in wing-backed chairs by the fire, a chessboard on the coffee table between them. One was a stranger to Chavasse, an old white-haired man in his seventies who wore gold-rimmed spectacles and studied the chessboard intently.

The other, at first sight, might have been any high Civil Service official. The well-cut, dark grey suit, the old Etonian tie, even the greying hair, all seemed a part of the familiar brand image.

It was only when he turned his head sharply and looked up that the difference became apparent. This was the face of no ordinary man. Here was a supremely intelligent being, with the cold grey eyes of a man who would be, above all things, a realist.

"I hear you've been looking for me," Chavasse said as he peeled off his wet trench coat.

The Chief smiled faintly. "That's putting it mildly. You must have found somewhere new."

Chavasse nodded. "The Caravel Club in Great Portland Street. They do a nice steak and there's a gaming room, chemmy and roulette mostly."

"Is it worth a visit?"

"Not really," Chavasse grinned. "Rather boring and too damned expensive. It's time I saw a little action of another kind."

"I think we can oblige you, Paul," the Chief said. "I'd like you to meet Professor Craig, by the way."

The old man shook hands and smiled. "So you're the language expert? I've heard a lot about you, young man."

"All to the good, I hope?" Chavasse took a cigarette from a box on the coffee table and pulled forward a chair.

"Professor Craig is chairman of the Joint Space Research Programme recently set up by NATO," the Chief said. "He's brought us rather an interesting problem. To be perfectly frank, I think you're the only available Bureau agent capable of handling it."

"Well, that's certainly a flattering beginning," Chavasse said. "What's the story?"

The Chief carefully inserted a Turkish cigarette into an elegent silver holder. "When were you last in Tibet, Paul?"

Chavasse frowned. "You know that as well as I

do. Three years ago, when we brought out the Dalai Lama."

"How would you feel about going in again?"

Chavasse shrugged. "My Tibetan is still pretty fair. Not fluent, but good enough. It's the other problems specific to the area which would worry me most. Mainly the fact that I'm a European, I suppose."

"But I understood you to say you'd helped out the Dalai Lama three years ago," Professor Craig said.

Chavasse nodded. "But that was different. Straight in and out again within a few days. I don't know how long I could get by if I was there for any period of time. I don't know if you're aware of this fact, Professor, but not a single Allied soldier escaped from a Chinese prison camp during the Korean War, and for obvious reasons. Drop me into Russia in suitable clothes and I could pass without question. In a street in Peking, I'd stick out like a sore thumb."

"Fair enough," the Chief said. "I appreciate your point, but what if we could get round it?"

"That would still leave the Chinese," Chavasse told him. "They've really tightened up since I was last there. Especially after the Tibetan revolt. Although mind you, I think their control of large areas must be pretty nominal." He hesitated and then went on, "This thing—is it important?"

The Chief nodded gravely. "Probably the biggest I've ever asked you to handle."

47

"You'd better tell me about it."

The Chief leaned back in his chair. "What would you say was the gravest international problem at the moment—the Bomb?"

Chavasse shook his head. "No, I don't think so. Not anymore, anyway. Probably the space race."

The Chief nodded. "I agree, and the fact that John Glenn and those who have followed him have successfully emulated Gagarin and Titov has got our Russian friends worried. The gap is narrowing—and they know it."

"Is there anything they can do about it?" Chavasse said.

The Chief nodded. "Indeed there is, and they've been working on it for too damned long already—but perhaps Professor Craig would like to tell you about it. He's the expert."

Professor Craig took off his spectacles and started to polish their lenses with the handkerchief from his breast pocket. "The great problem is propulsion, Mr. Chavasse. Bigger and better rockets just aren't the answer, not when it comes to travelling to the moon, and anything farther involves immense distances."

"And presumably the Russians have got something?" Chavasse said.

Craig shook his head. "Not yet, but I think they may be very near it. Since 1956, they've been experimenting with an ionic rocket drive using energy emitted by stars as the motive force."

"It sounds rather like something out of a science-fiction story," Chavasse said.

"I only wish it were, young man," Professor Craig said gravely. "Unfortunately it's hard fact, and if we don't come up with another answer quickly we might as well throw in the towel."

"And presumably, there *is* another answer?" Chavasse said softly.

The professor adjusted his spectacles carefully and nodded. "In normal circumstances, I would have said no, but in view of certain information which has recently come into my hands, it would appear that there is still a chance for us."

The Chief leaned forward. "Ten days ago, a young Tibetan nobleman arrived in Srinagar, the capital of Kashmir. Ferguson, our local man, took him in charge. Besides possessing valuable information about the state of things in western Tibet at the present time, he was also carrying a letter for Professor Craig. It was from Karl Hoffner."

Chavasse frowned. "I've heard of him vaguely. Wasn't he some kind of medical missionary in Tibet for years?"

The Chief nodded. "A very wonderful man whom most people have completely forgotten. Remarkably similar career to Albert Schweitzer. Doctor, musician, philosopher, mathematician. He's given forty years of his life to Tibet."

"And he's still alive?" Chavasse said.

The Chief nodded. "Living in a small town called Changu about one hundred and fifty miles across the border from Kashmir. Under house arrest, as far as we can make out."

"This letter," Chavasse said, turning to Professor Craig. "Why was it addressed to you?"

"Karl Hoffner and I were fellow students and research workers for years." Craig sighed heavily. "One of the great minds of the century, Mr. Chavasse. He could have had all the fame of an Einstein, but he chose to bury himself in a forgotten country."

"But what was in the letter that was so interesting?" Chavasse asked.

"On the face of it, nothing very much. It was simply a letter from one old friend to another. He'd apparently heard that this young Tibetan was making a break for it and decided to take the opportunity of writing to me, probably for the last time. He's in poor health."

"How are they treating him?"

"Apparently quite well." Craig shrugged. "He was always greatly loved by the people. Probably the Communists are using him as a sort of symbol. He said in his letter that he had been confined to his house for more than a year and to help pass the time had returned to his greatest love, mathematics."

"Presumably this is important?"

"Karl Hoffner is probably one of the great

mathematicians of all time," Professor Craig said solemnly. "Do you mind if I get a little technical?"

"By all means," Chavasse told him.

"I don't know the extent of your knowledge of mathematical concepts," Craig said, "but you are perhaps aware that Einstein demonstrated that matter is nothing but energy fixed in a rigid pattern?"

"E equals mc squared." Chavasse grinned. "I'm with you so far."

"In a celebrated thesis written for his doctorate while a young man," Craig went on, "Karl Hoffner demonstrated that energy itself is *space* locked up in a certain pattern. His proof involved an audacious development of non-Euclidean geometry which was as revolutionary as Einstein's theory of relativity."

51

"Now, you've completely lost me," Chavasse said.

"It doesn't matter." Craig smiled. "Probably only six brains on earth were capable of understanding his theory at the time, such was its complexity. It aroused considerable interest in academic circles and was then virtually forgotten. It was only theoretical, you see. It led nowhere and had no conceivable practical application."

"And now he's taken it one stage further," Chavasse said. "Is that what you're leading up to?"

Craig nodded. "He mentioned in his letter,

quite casually I might add, that he had reached the solution to the problem. He has proved that space can be twisted, manipulated if you like, until it becomes an energy field."

"And this is really important?" Chavasse said.

"Important?" The professor sighed. "For one thing, it relegates nuclear physics to roughly the Eocene Age of science. For another, it gives us an entirely new concept of space travel. We could produce an energy drive for our rockets from space itself, something that would be infinitely superior to the Russian concept of the ionic drive."

"Do you think Hoffner has any idea of the important of his discovery?" Chavasse said.

Craig shook his head. "Given his circumstances, I don't think he is even aware that orbital flights have taken place. If he knew that man had already crossed the space threshold, the value of his discovery would be at once obvious to him."

"It's incredible," Chavasse said. "Quite incredible."

"What's even more to the point is that knowing this does us no damn good at all as long as the know-how remains locked in the brain of a sick old man under house arrest in a Communist-dominated country," the Chief said. "We've got to get him out, Paul."

Chavasse sighed. "Well, I was begging for action," he said, "and now I've got it, though how the hell I'm supposed to pull it off, I don't know."

"I've already given that quite some thought." The Chief pushed the chessboard out of the way and unfolded a large map.

"Now this is the area involved—Kashmir and western Tibet. Changu is about a hundred and fifty miles from the border. You'll notice that some fifty miles into Tibet, there's a village called Rudok. In his despatch the other day, Ferguson had already informed me that, according to the young Tibetan nobleman who brought out the letter, the Chinese have little control of the area. He says the monastery outside Rudok is quite a centre of resistance. If we could get you there, you'd at least have a base. Of course, from then on, you'd have to play it by ear."

"Two obvious points," Chavasse said. "How do I get in and how do I get the locals to accept me if I do?"

"That's all arranged," the Chief said. "Since yesterday evening when Professor Craig first came to me to point out that there was more in the letter than met the eye, I've used the special line to speak to Ferguson in Srinagar no fewer than four times. He's arranged for this young Tibetan to go in with you."

"And what about transportation?"

"We'll fly you in."

Chavasse frowned. "Are you sure it's possible

53

from Kashmir? The Ladakh range is a hell of a height."

"Ferguson's dug up a bush pilot named Jan Kerensky. He's a Pole—flew for the R.A.F. during the war. He's doing government work in the area, aerial reconnaissance and so forth. Apparently, there's an old R.A.F. emergency airstrip outside Leh which he sometimes uses. That's only eighty or ninety miles from the Tibetan border. We've offered him five thousand to fly you in and land you at this monastery near Rudok and another five to pick you up again exactly one week later."

"Does he think he can do it?"

The Chief nodded. "He says it's possible, no more than that. You're obviously going to need a hell of a lot of luck."

"You can say that again," Chavasse told him. "When do I go?"

"There's a Vulcan bomber leaving R.A.F. Edgeworth at nine for Singapore. It'll drop you off at Aden. You can fly on to Kashmir from there."

The Chief got to his feet and said briskly, "I don't think there's anything more we can do here, Professor. I'll take you home. You look as if you could do with some sleep."

As Craig started to get up, Chavasse said quickly, "Just a moment, Professor, if you don't mind." Craig sat down again and Chavasse went on, "There's always the question of how I'm to identify myself to Doctor Hoffner. I've got to

54

make him believe beyond a shadow of a doubt that I'm absolutely genuine. Can you suggest anything?"

Craig stared into space for a moment, a slight frown on his face, and then, quite suddenly, he smiled. "There is something in Karl Koffner's past which only he and I know," he said. "We were in love with the same girl. There was a certain May evening at his rooms in Cambridge when we decided to settle the matter once and for all. She was sitting in the garden and on the toss of a coin, Karl went out to her first. I'll never forget the look on his face when he returned. Later, as I stood in the garden with her after she'd promised to become my wife, he sat in the darkness inside and played the *Moonlight Sonata*. He was a superb pianist."

"Thank you, sir," Chavasse said gently.

"A long, long time ago, young man, but he'll remember every detail of that night. I know I do." Craig stood up and held out his hand. "I can only wish you luck, Mr. Chavasse. I hope to see you again, very soon."

As Craig picked up his coat, the Chief turned to Chavasse briskly and smiled. "Well, Paul, it's going to be a tough one, but just remember how important this is to all of us. Jean's going to stay and cook you a meal and so on. She'll drive you to Edgeworth and see you off. Sorry I can't come myself, but I've an important conference at the Foreign Office at nine-thirty."

"That's all right, sir," Chavasse said.

The Chief ushered Craig to the door, opened it and turned. He seemed to be about to say something else and then thought better of it and closed the door gently behind him.

Chavasse stood in the middle of the room for a long moment after they had gone, and then he lit a cigarette and went back into the kitchen.

Jean Frazer was making a bacon and egg fry. She turned and wrinkled her nose. "Better have a shower. You look awful."

"So would you if you'd been handed a job like this," he said. "What's happened to the coffee, anyway?"

"I didn't want to disturb you." She hesitated and came towards him, smoothing her palms nervously along her thighs. "It's not so good, is it, Paul?"

"It shines," he said. "Putting it mildly." He grinned crookedly. "Sometimes I wonder why I ever got mixed up in this crazy business."

Suddenly, she seemed close to tears. He bent down quickly and kissed her on the mouth. "Give me ten minutes to shower and change and I'll have breakfast with you. Afterwards, you can drive me to my doom."

She turned away quickly and he went back into the living room and started to take off his tie. He opened the window and stood there for a moment, breathing in the raw freshness of the rain, and suddenly he felt exhilarated—tremendously exhilarated. It was the first time in two months that he had felt really alive. When he went into the bathroom, he was whistling.

INDIA
TIBET
·····················
1962

4

When Chavasse crossed the tarmac at Srinagar airport the following morning, Ferguson was waiting by the gate, a tall, greying man in his middle forties who looked cool and immaculate in a white linen suit.

He grinned and shook hands. "It's been a long time, Paul. How are you?"

Chavasse was tired and his suit looked as if it had been slept in, but he managed a smile. "Bloody awful. I caught my flight out of Aden on time, but we ran into an electric storm and I missed my connection in Delhi. Had to hang around for hours waiting for a plane out."

"What you need is a shower and a stiff drink," Ferguson told him. "Any luggage?"

"I'm travelling light this trip." Chavasse held

up his canvas grip. "I'm relying on you to supply me with the sort of outfit I'm going to need."

"I've already got it in hand," Ferguson said. "Let's get out of here. My car's parked just outside."

As they drove into Srinagar, Chavasse lit a cigarette and looked out the window at the great white peaks of the mountains, outlined like a jagged frieze against the vivid blue sky. "So this is the Vale of Kashmir?"

"Disappointed?" said Ferguson.

"On the contrary," Chavasse told him. "None of the books I've read do it justice. How long have you been here?"

"About eighteen months." Ferguson grinned. "Oh, I know I've been put out to pasture, but I'm not complaining. I'm strictly a deskman from now on."

"How's the leg these days?"

Ferguson shrugged. "Could be worse. Sometimes I imagine it's still there, but they say that kind of hallucination can last for years."

They slowed down as the car nosed its way carefully through the narrow streets of a bazaar, and Chavasse looked out into the milling crowd and thought about Ferguson. A good, efficient agent, one of the best the Bureau had until someone had tossed that grenade through his bedroom window one dark night in Algiers. It was the sort of thing that could have happened to anybody. No matter how good you were, or how careful, sooner or later your number came out of the box.

He pushed the thought away and lit another cigarette. "This flier you've dug up—Kerensky? Is he reliable?"

"One of the best pilots I've ever come across," Ferguson said. "Squadron leader in the R.A.F. during the war, decorated by everybody in sight. He's been out here for about five years."

"How's he doing?"

"Can't go wrong, really. This mountain flying is pretty tricky; he doesn't exactly have to worry about competition."

"And he thinks he can fly me in?"

Ferguson grinned. "For the kind of money we're paying him, he'd have a pretty good try at a round trip to hell. He's that kind of man."

"Does he live here in Srinagar?"

Ferguson nodded. "Has a houseboat on the river. Only five minutes from my place, as a matter of fact."

They were driving out through the other side of the city, and now Ferguson slowed and turned the car into the driveway of a pleasant, white-painted bungalow. A houseboy in scarlet turban and white drill ran down the steps from the verandah and relieved Chavasse of the canvas grip.

Inside it was cool and dark, with venetian blinds covering the windows, and Ferguson led the way into a bathroom that was white-tiled and gleaming, startling in its modernity.

"I think you'll find everything you need," he said. "I've told the boy to lay out some fresh clothes for you. I'll be on the terrace."

When Ferguson had gone, Chavasse examined himself in the mirror. His eyes were slightly bloodshot, his face was lined with fatigue, and he badly needed a shave. He sighed heavily and started to undress.

When he went out on the terrace twenty minutes later, dressed in cotton slacks and a clean white shirt, his hair still damp from the shower, he felt like a different man. Ferguson sat at a small table shaded by a gaudy umbrella. Beneath the terrace, the garden ran all the way down to the River Jhelum.

"Quite a view you've got," Chavasse said.

Ferguson nodded. "It's even nicer in the evening. When the sun goes down over the mountains, it's quite a sight, believe me."

The houseboy appeared, holding a tray on which stood two tall glasses beaded with frosted moisture. Chavasse picked one up, took a quick swallow and sighed with pleasure. "That's all I needed. Now I feel human again."

"We aim to please," Ferguson said. "Would you like something to eat?"

"I had a meal on the plane," Chavasse said.

"I'd like to see Kerensky as soon as possible, if that's all right with you."

"Suits me," Ferguson said, and rose to his feet and led the way down a flight of shallow stone steps to the sunbaked lawn.

As they passed through a wicker gate and turned on to the towpath, Chavasse said, "What about the Tibetan? What's he like?"

"Joro?" Ferguson said. "I think you'll be impressed. He's about thirty, remarkably intelligent and speaks good English. Apparently, Hoffner arranged for him to spend three years at a mission school in Delhi when he was a kid. He thinks the world of the old man."

"Where is he now?"

"Living in an encampment outside the city with some fellow countrymen. Plenty of refugees trailing into Kashmir from across the border these days." He pointed suddenly. "There's Kerensky now."

The red and gold houseboat was moored to the riverbank about forty yards away. The man who stood on the cabin roof was wearing only bathing shorts. As Ferguson and Chavasse approached, he dived cleanly into the water.

Ferguson negotiated the narrow gangplank with some difficulty because of his leg, so Chavasse took the lead and gave him a hand down to the deck. It had been scrubbed to a dazzling whiteness; in fact, the whole boat was in beautiful condition.

"What's it like below?" Chavasse asked.

"First-rate!" Ferguson told him. "A lot of people spend their vacation in one of these things every year."

Several cane chairs and a table were grouped under an awning by the stern and they sat down and waited for Kerensky, who had seen them and was returning to the boat in a fast, but effortless, crawl. He pulled himself over the rail, water streaming from his squat, powerful body, and grinned. "Ah, Mr. Ferguson, the man with all the money. I was beginning to give you up."

"My friend missed his plane in Delhi," Ferguson told him.

Jan Kerensky had an engagingly ugly face topped by a stubble of iron grey hair, and when he smiled, his skin creased in a thousand wrinkles. "I hope he's got strong nerves." He turned to Chavasse. "You're going to need them where we're going."

Chavasse took an instant liking to the man. "According to Ferguson I couldn't be in better hands."

Kerensky's teeth flashed in a wide grin. "I'm inclined to agree with him, but you'd better reserve your judgment. Excuse me a moment."

He padded across the deck and vanished below. "Quite a character," Chavasse said.

"And then some," Ferguson said. "If anyone can get you there, he can."

When Kerensky came back on deck, he carried

a tray of drinks and a large, folded map. He placed the tray on the table and sat down. "Iced vodka, my friends. The best drink in the world."

Chavasse took a long swallow. "Polish, isn't it?"

"But of course," Kerensky told him. "Only the best for Kerensky. A man needs it in this climate to help keep him in shape." He slapped his brawny chest with one hand. "Not bad for forty-five, eh, Mr. Chavasse?"

Chavasse managed to keep his face straight, but it was quite an effort. "I'm impressed."

Kerensky pushed the tray out of the way and unfolded the map. "Let's get down to business. Ferguson says you've been inside Tibet before?"

"Only the southeast," Chavasse told him.

"The west is different," Kerensky said. "Nearly all of it is fifteen, maybe sixteen thousand feet above sea level. Wild, rugged country."

"And you think we can fly in?"

Kerensky shrugged. "We can try. There's an emergency strip at Leh which I sometimes use. That's a village in the gorge of the upper Indus about eleven thousand feet up. From there to Rudok is only a hundred and twenty miles."

"And can we land there all right?"

Kerensky nodded. "I've already had a talk with this Tibetan who's going with you. He's described a perfect spot about eight miles east of Rudok. A sand flat beside a lake."

"That sounds fine," Chavasse said. "What kind of plane are you using?"

"A de Havilland Beaver. Only a small, light plane with good maneuverability stands a chance in these mountains," Kerensky said. "We'll cross into Tibet through the Pangong Tso Pass. That's maybe fifteen thousand feet up, so I'll be scraping her belly. No picnic, I'm warning you, and there's plenty of snow and ice up there. If you feel like backing out, say the word now."

"And spoil your fun?" Chavasse said. "When do we leave?"

Kerensky grinned. "You know, I like you, my friend. Almost, I am persuaded to do this job for love, but my mercenary nature triumphs as usual. We'll fly up to Leh this afternoon. There's a full moon tonight. If the sky is clear, we can try for Rudok straightaway, but we can't chance the passes through the mountains if there is cloud."

"How does that suit you, Paul?" Ferguson said.

Chavasse shrugged. "The sooner we go, the sooner we're back, as far as I'm concerned. What time?"

"Let's make it three o'clock at the airport," Kerensky said. "What about the Tibetan?"

"We're going to see him now," Ferguson told him. "I'll arrange to have him there on time."

They all stood up and Kerensky raised his glass in a toast. "As we say in my country, may we go to a good death."

For a moment, his face was serious, and then he emptied his glass and grinned. "And now, if you gentlemen will excuse me, I'd like to finish my swim."

He turned and dived over the rail into the yellow water and Chavasse and Ferguson crossed the gangplank to the shore and walked back to the bungalow.

Driving out of Srinager towards the refugee encampment to see Joro a little while later, Ferguson was silent, a slight frown on his face.

"What's eating you?" Chavasse asked him.

Ferguson shrugged. "Oh, it's probably nothing. It's just that I get the impression Kerensky isn't anything like so happy about this affair as he'd like to pretend."

"For the kind of money he's being paid, he doesn't need to be happy," Chavasse said. "On the other hand, he had a hell of a war. Probably worried about taking the hitcher to the well too often."

"And you, Paul." Ferguson glanced sideways at him. "What about you?"

"You should know better than to ask a question like that," Chavasse said. "I go where the Bureau sends me. This is just another job as far as I'm concerned. Perhaps a little tougher than most, but that's all."

"But doesn't the thought of going in there worry you?" Ferguson persisted.

"Sure it does." Chavasse grinned. "If it didn't, I wouldn't go."

Ferguson turned the car off the highway and they followed a dirt road for several miles. They were moving up through the lowlands, climbing high into grassy meadows, when suddenly they topped a small rise and saw twenty or thirty tents below, beside a small stream.

It was a peaceful scene, with the smoke of the cooking fires rising straight in the calm air. Several women stood knee-deep in the stream washing clothing, their long woollen *shubas* tucked into their belts, and barefooted children played a noisy game of hide-and-seek.

The tents were typically Tibetan and consisted of yak skins sewn together and stretched over a round wickerwork frame which was surrounded by a low wall of stones or turves.

The camp had a primitive, quiet charm, and Chavasse smiled as a young boy noticed their approach and called to his friends. A moment later, the whole pack of them surged forward, calling excitedly to their mothers down at the stream.

The women looked up, shading their eyes against the sun, and at that moment a horseman galloped over the crest of a hill fifty or sixty yards away, scattering a group of grazing yaks, and rode down into the camp.

He wore a long, wide-sleeved robe and sheepskin *shuba* which left his chest bare to the waist, and knee-length boots of untanned hide that had been dyed green. His hair was coiled into plaits on either side and covered by a conical sheepskin hat. There was a large silver ring in his left ear.

He reined in his small Tibetan horse, dismounted and came towards them, a strangely medieval figure. He was tall and muscular, and his deeply tanned face was not in the least oriental. His high cheekbones and aquiline nose gave him a definitely aristocratic air and the children, who quickly parted to let him through, ducked their heads in respect as he passed.

"Joro," Ferguson said. "This is Mr. Chavasse."

The Tibetan held out his hand. "I am glad you are here," he said simply.

Chavasse was impressed. Joro's English was excellent, but there was more to it than that. He was a man who would have stood out in any company. He looked intelligent and tough, every inch a leader—not at all the sort of man who would run away from a fight. Chavasse was intrigued.

They walked a little way out of the camp and sat down on a grassy bank. Chavasse offered Joro a cigarette, which he accepted, and took one himself. As he gave the Tibetan a light, he said, "Ferguson tells me you're willing to return to Tibet and to help me as much as you can. Why?"

"For two reasons," Joro said. "Because Mr. Ferguson has told me that you were one of those who helped the Dalai Lama to escape, and because you wish to help Dr. Hoffner."

"But why did you leave Tibet in the first place? Were you in trouble?"

Joro shook his head. "I was not a suspected person, if that's what you mean. No, Mr. Chavasse. My people are brave, but we can't fight the Chinese with broadswords and muskets. We need modern rifles and machine guns. I came through the Pangong Tso Pass with gold in the lining of my *shuba*. I came to buy arms, and Mr. Ferguson has arranged this for me."

"You'll be taking them in with you," Ferguson said. "It's all fixed up. Some rifles and ammunition, a couple of submachine guns and a box of grenades. It's all I could manage. We've just come from Kerensky. He wants to fly to Leh this afternoon. Is that all right with you?"

Joro nodded. "I see no reason for delay if Mr. Chavasse is ready."

"If the weather is good, Kerensky wants to try for Rudok tonight," Chavasse said, "so we haven't got much time. You'd better fill me in on a few things. What's the general state of affairs in western Tibet?"

"Very different from the rest of the country. The Chinese have built a road to link Gartok and Yarkand through the disputed territory of the Aksai Chin Plateau, which they claim from India, but there is little traffic. The area is the most sparsely populated part of Tibet, and they only control the villages and towns, and not all of those."

"So there's been some local resistance?"

Joro smiled faintly. "Most of my people are herdsmen who move constantly with their flocks, hard mountaineers who do not take kindly to Chinese brutality. What would you expect?"

"I thought that as Buddhists, the Tibetans were generally against any kind of violence?" Ferguson remarked.

"That was true once," Joro said grimly, "but then the Reds came to butcher our young men and defile our women. Before the Lord Buddha brought the way of peace to us, we Tibetans were warriors. The Chinese have made us warriors again."

"He's right," Chavasse told Ferguson. "When I was in the south, even the monks were fighting."

"That is so," Joro said. "Near Rudok at the monastery of Yalung Gompa we shall find many friends. The monks will help us in any way they can."

"Now tell me about Hoffner," Chavasse said. "What shape was he in when you last saw him?"

"He had been very ill. That was why I went to see him. I told him I intended to visit Kashmir and he asked me to take the letter for him."

"He's not closely guarded then?"

Joro shook his head. "He is allowed to continue living in his old house at Changu, which is

73

an ancient walled town of perhaps five thousand people. The Chinese commandant for the entire area lives there, Colonel Li."

"And Hoffner is confined to his house?"

"He occasionally walked in the streets, but he is forbidden to leave the town." Joro shrugged. "They don't bother to guard him closely, if that's what you want to know. Where would he go, a frail old man?"

"That means we can probably work something out without too much difficulty," Chavasse said. "After all, we'll only have to get him from Changu to this landing ground you've found near Rudok, and then Kerensky can take over."

"There may be difficulties you have not foreseen," Juro said. "For instance, there is Hoffner's housekeeper. She may prove awkward. She was not there on the last occasion I saw Hoffner, but I believe she is still with him, and I don't trust her."

"Why not?" Chavasse asked.

"For the best of all possible reasons," Joro told him. "She is Chinese—or rather her mother was. Her father was Russian, which is as bad. Her name is Katya Stranoff. She had been travelling with her father from Sinkiang to Lhasa, and he died on the way."

"And Hoffner took her in?"

Joro nodded. "It is his great fault that he must always help others, no matter what the cost to himself."

Chavasse thought about it for a moment, a frown on his face. Finally he said, "What it comes down to is this: You don't trust her, but you've nothing concrete to go on. For all we know, she may be perfectly harmless?"

"That is so," Joro said reluctantly.

"Then we'll have to take a chance on her. When we get to the monastery, you'll have to go to Changu anyway to spy out the land for me. But we can sort all that out later."

Ferguson got to his feet. "If that's all for the moment, we'd better be getting back to Srinagar. I've got plenty to arrange before that plane takes off, and you could use the time to catch up on a little sleep, Paul."

Chavasse nodded. "That's the best idea you've had yet." He smiled and shook hands with Joro. "Until this afternoon then."

They left him sitting on the grassy bank and walked back through the camp to the car. As they drove away, Ferguson said, "What did you think of him?"

"He was everything you said he was and then some. I couldn't have wished for a better companion."

"I must say that after listening to what he had to say, the whole thing looks as if it might be rather easier than I thought," Ferguson said. "Of course there's this woman he mentioned, but she's probably harmless."

"Probably," Chavasse agreed, and sighed.

There always seemed to be a woman around somewhere, and this one was the unknown quantity with a vengeance. However, time would tell. He eased himself into a comfortable position in the seat, tilted his hat forward and closed his eyes.

5

It had stopped raining and a white band of moonlight sprawled across the bed. Chavasse lay in that half-world between sleeping and waking and stared up through the gloom at the ceiling.

After a while, he glanced at his watch. It was almost eleven o'clock. He lay back against the pillow for a moment longer, his body wet with perspiration, and then lifted the blankets aside and slipped out of bed. He quickly dried his body on a towel and dressed, pulling a thick, woollen sweater over his head before opening the window and stepping out onto the terrace.

The flat-roofed houses of Leh straggled down to the Indus below; the immense walls of the gorge were dark shadows against the sky. It was peaceful and quiet, the only sound a dog barking somewhere across the river, his voice a muted bell in the night.

Chavasse lit a cigarette, his hands cupped against the wind. As he flicked away the match, a bank of cloud rolled away from the moon and the countryside was bathed in a hard white light. The night sky was incredibly beautiful, with stars strung away to the horizon, where the mountain lifted uneasily to meet them.

He inhaled the freshness of the earth, wet after the rain, and wondered why everything couldn't be as simple and uncomplicated as this. You only had to stand and look at it and it cost you nothing except a little time and it gave so much.

And then a small wind touched him coldly on the cheek, sending a wave of greyness through him, reminding him that half an hour's flying time away through the darkness was the border. The wind called to him as it moaned across the rooftops, and he turned and went inside.

The hotel was wrapped in quiet and as he went downstairs, a blast of hot, stale air met him from the small hall where an ancient fan creaked uselessly in the ceiling, hardly causing a movement in the atmosphere.

The Hindu night clerk was asleep at his desk, head propped between his hands, and Chavasse moved softly past him and went into the bar.

Kerensky sat at a table by the window, a napkin tucked under his chin. He was the only customer, and a waiter hovered nearby and watched with awe as the Pole steadily demolished the large roasted chicken on his plate.

Chavasse went behind the bar, poured himself a large Scotch and added ice water. As he crossed to where Kerensky sat, the Pole looked up and grinned.

"Ah, there you are. I was just going to have you wakened. What about something to eat?"

Chavasse shook his head. "Nothing for me, thanks."

"How do you feel?" Kerensky asked.

"Fine." Chavasse stood at the window and looked out across the terrace into the moonlight. "It's certainly the right night for it."

"Couldn't have been better." Kerensky chuckled. "In this moonlight, I can fly through the passes with no trouble, and that was always the most dangerous part of the operation. It's going to be a piece of cake."

"I hope you're right," Chavasse said.

"But I always am. During the war I flew over one hundred operations. Every time something bad happened, I felt lousy beforehand. Through my grandmother on my mother's side, I have Gypsy blood. I always know, I assure you, and tonight I feel good."

He leaned over and poured vodka into Chavasse's empty glass. "Drink up and we'll go to the airstrip. I sent Joro up there an hour ago with my local man."

Chavasse looked down into his glass, a slight

frown on his face. Somewhere in his being, a primitive instinct, perhaps that slight mystical element common to all ancient races and inherited from his Breton ancestors, told him that it was no good. In spite of what Kerensky said, it was no good!

Accepting that fact, he was taken possession of by a strange fatalistic calm. He raised his glass and smiled and took the vodka down in one easy swallow.

"I'm ready when you are," he said.

The airstrip was half a mile outside Leh on a flat plain beside the river. It was not an official stopping place for any of the big airlines and had been constructed by the R.A.F. as an emergency strip during the war.

There was one prefabricated concrete hangar still painted in the grey-green camouflage of wartime, and rainwater dripped steadily through its sagging roof as they went inside.

The plane squatted in the middle of the hangar, the scarlet and silver of its fuselage gleaming in the light thrown out by two hurricane lamps suspended from the rafters. Jagbar, Kerensky's mechanic, was sitting at the controls, a look of intense concentration on his face as he listened to the sound of the engine. Joro was sitting beside him.

Jagbar jumped down to the ground and Joro

followed him. "How does it sound?" Kerensky said.

Jagbar grinned, exposing stained and decaying teeth. "Perfect, sahib."

"And fuel?"

"I've filled her to capacity, including the emergency tank."

Kerensky nodded and patted the side of the plane. "Fly well for me, angel," he crooned in Polish, and turned to Chavasse. "I'm ready when you are."

Chavasse looked at the Tibetan and smiled. "I'll have my disguise now, such as it is."

Joro nodded and pulled a bundle out of the plane. It contained a brown woollen robe, a sheepskin *shuba* and cap and a pair of Tibetan boots in untanned hide.

Chavasse changed quickly and turned to Kerensky. "Will I do?"

The Pole nodded. "At a distance, no one would look at you twice, but remember to keep that face covered. It's as Gallic as a packet of Gauloises or the Pigalle on a Saturday night. Distinctly out of keeping with the Tibetan steppes."

Chavasse grinned. "I'll try to remember that."

He and Joro climbed into the plane first, and then Kerensky slipped into the pilot's seat. He opened the map and turned to Joro.

"You're sure about that border patrol?"

The Tibetan nodded confidently. "They are

supposed to patrol daily to the Pangong Tso Pass, but lately it has been unsafe for them to do so. There are only ten men and a sergeant. They stay pretty close to Rudok."

Kerensky leaned down to Jagbar. "Look for me in about two hours."

The mechanic nodded and pulled the chocks away; Kerensky taxied slowly out of the hangar and turned into the wind. A moment later, the end of the airstrip was rushing to meet them. He pulled the stick back and the plane lifted into the gorge, rock walls flashing by on either side.

The mountains rose to meet them, gigantic and awe-inspiring, and they climbed higher and swung in a gentle curve that carried them between twin peaks and into another pass.

The rock walls were uncomfortably close, and Chavasse turned away hurriedly and looked for something to do. Joro was sitting with one of the submachine guns on his knee, carefully loading spare clips from a box of ammunition.

Chavasse took out his own weapon, a Walther, and checked its action—not that a handgun would be of much use to him if he ran into real trouble. He slipped it back into the soft leather holster at his hip and reached for the other submachine gun.

Within half an hour, they seemed lost in a landscape so barren, it might have been the moon. Great snow-covered peaks towered on every side and Kerensky, handling the plane with genius, moved through a maze that seemed to have no ending. Beyond the peaks, the stars were like diamond chips set in a black velvet cushion, brighter than Chavasse had ever known.

On several occasions, they dropped in air pockets. Once, as they curved from one pass into another, Chavasse could have sworn that their right wingtip touched the rock wall, but they flew on, Kerensky's great hands steady on the controls.

Suddenly, they skimmed over the shoulder of a mountain and three hundred feet below, a lake glittered in the moonlight.

"Pangong Tso!" Joro shouted above the roar of the engine.

The great pass lifted to meet them. Kerensky eased back the stick slightly, but as the plane rose, so did the frozen earth beneath.

Chavasse held his breath and waited for the crash, but it didn't come. With fifty feet to spare, they were over the hump and flashing between rock walls on one side and a glacier on the other.

Beneath them, a dark plateau rolled away into the distance as far as the eye could see. Kerensky turned and smiled in the dim light thrown out by the instrument panel. "Thought you might like to know we're now over Tibet," he shouted. "I'm altering course slightly to bypass Rudok. No sense in advertising."

The plane banked sharply to the east and then

resumed level flight. The view was spectacular as the rolling steppes stretched away to the horizon. Here and there, hollows and valleys lay dark and forbidding, thrown into relief by the white moonlight, which picked out the higher stretches of ground.

And then a lake appeared, and a few moments later, another. Joro tapped Kerensky on the shoulder and the Pole nodded and took the plane down.

The sand flat at the eastern end of the lake gleamed white in the moonlight and Kerensky circled once and started to put the plane's nose down for a landing. Suddenly he banked sharply and started to climb.

"What's wrong?" Chavasse cried.

"Thought I saw a light down there," Kerensky said. "Just over the hill from the shore. I'll go down and take a look."

He took the plane round once more, but there was no sign of a light. "What do you think?" he said over his shoulder.

Chavasse looked enquiringly at Joro and the Tibetan shrugged. "If there was a light, it could only have been a herdsman's fire. Chinese soldiers wouldn't dare to spend a night in the open in this area."

"That settles it." Chavasse tapped Kerensky on the shoulder. "Put her down."

Kerenksy nodded and circled the lake once more before turning into the wind for a perfect landing on the shore. Chavasse didn't waste any time. As the plane taxied to a halt, he opened the door, jumped to the ground and turned to help Joro down with the guns and ammunition.

Sand, whipped up by the propeller, enveloped him in a cloud of stinging particles, but within a few moments the boxes were on the ground and Joro was beside him.

Kerenksy reached over to close the door. "One week from now, same time, same place," he shouted above the roar of the engine. "And be here on time. I don't want to hang around."

Chavasse and Joro quickly dragged the boxes out of the way and stood back and watched as Kerenksy taxied along to the other end of the strand and turned into the wind.

As he moved forward, the engine note deepened, and a few moments later the plane banked away across the lake, gaining height all the time, and disappeared towards the northwest.

His ears still ringing with the sound of the plane's engine, Chavasse turned to Joro. "We'd better find somewhere to dump this little lot until your pals from Yalung Gompa can pick it up."

He moved across the sand towards a narrow gully which cut into the side of the hill about forty yards away. Strange how the sound of the engine still rang in his ears, but the gully looked just the place.

He turned to call Joro and a jeep appeared on the crest of the hill as if by magic.

In that first frozen moment of panic he was aware of the peak caps of the soldiers and the long ugly barrel of the machine gun mounted on a swivel, and then he was running into the open, one hand reaching for his Walther.

"Look out, Joro," he cried in English.

The heavy barrel of the machine gun was already swinging towards the Tibetan, and ribbons of fire stabbed through the night, kicking up the sand in great fountains.

Joro flung himself sideways, rolling desperately, and Chavasse dropped to one knee and got off a couple of shots to draw their fire.

Joro scrambled to his feet and disappeared into the shelter of a jumbled mass of boulders at the water's edge as the barrel of the machine gun turned towards Chavasse. He retreated into the mouth of the gully, flinging himself flat on his face as bullets hammered the rocks beside him.

A splinter cut his cheek and when he got to his feet and tried to move farther into the sheltering darkness, a bullet sliced across his left shoulder.

He hugged the earth again and waited and when the bullets at last stopped coming, the silence was even harder to bear. He cautiously scrambled to his feet again, and immediately there was a muffled explosion and the gully was bathed in a hard white light.

He looked up at the descending flare and

waited, because there was no place to run to. After a while, stones rattled down and two Chinese soldiers appeared on the rim of the gully, burp guns ready. As he raised the Walther to fire, a third man appeared between them.

He stood on the edge of the gully, a slight smile on his face, so close that Chavasse could see the feather in his Tyrolean hat and the fur collar of his hunting jacket.

"Don't be a damned fool," the man said calmly in English. "That thing's going to do you no good at all."

Chavasse looked up at him in astonishment and then, in spite of the pain in his shoulder, he laughed. It had, after all, been a night for surprises.

"You know, I think you've got something there," he said, and tossed the Walther across and waited for them to come for him.

6

The wind from the steppes moved down into the hollow, touching Chavasse with icy fingers. He shivered and pulled his sheepskin *shuba* up about his face with one hand.

The pain in his shoulder had lapsed into a slow, dull ache, the raw flesh anesthetized by the bitter cold, and he had a splitting headache and a slight feeling of nausea. Probably something to do with the fact that he hadn't had sufficient time to become acclimatised to the altitude.

He sat with his back propped against one of the wheels of the jeep and a few feet away, a spirit stove flared in the wind in front of a small pup tent. The two Chinese soldiers crouched beside it. One of them held his burp gun across his knees and smoked a cigarette while the other heated coffee in an aluminum pan.

Chavasse wondered about Joro. At least he'd managed to get away in one piece, so something had been salvaged from the mess, but for the moment, he could look for no help in that direction. Without arms and alone, the Tibetan could accomplish nothing. If he managed to contact some of his men, that would be another story.

The tent flap opened and the man in the Tyrolean hat and hunting jacket crawled out carrying a first-aid box.

He crouched down beside Chavasse and grinned sympathetically. "How do you feel?"

Chavasse shrugged. "I'll survive, if that's what you mean."

The man produced a packet of cigarettes. "Try one of these. It might help."

He was about thirty-five, tall and well-built, and the match flared in his cupped hands to reveal a strong, sensitive face and mobile mouth.

Chavasse drew smoke deep into his lungs and coughed as it caught at the back of his throat. "Russian!" he exclaimed, holding the cigarette up, and suddenly things became a little clearer.

"But certainly." The man smiled. "Andrei Sergeievich Kurbsky at your service."

"I hope you won't be offended if I don't return the compliment."

"Perfectly understandable." Kurbsky laughed

good-naturedly. "Rather bad luck for you, our happening along when we did."

"Come to think of it, what are you doing out here at night anyway?" Chavasse demanded. "I understood this was a bad security area."

"I was on my way to Changu. Our engine broke down and by the time we'd diagnosed the trouble, it was dark so I decided to camp here for the night. It was quite a surprise when you flew in. Almost as great as when I heard you cry a warning to your comrade in English."

"I must be getting old." Chavasse sighed. "So it was your light we saw?"

Kurbsky nodded. "You interrupted my supper. Of course, I turned off the spirit stove as soon as you appeared. You obviously intended to land, and I didn't want to discourage you."

"And we thought it was a herdsman's fire," Chavasse told him bitterly.

"The fortunes of war, my friend." Kurbsky opened the first-aid box. "And now, if you're ready, I'll see what state you're in."

"It's only a scratch," Chavasse said. "The bullet ploughed a furrow across my shoulder, that's all."

The Russian examined the wound and then expertly bandaged it with a field dressing.

"You seem to know your stuff," Chavasse told him.

Kurbsky grinned. "I was a war correspondent in Korea. A hard school."

"And what are you doing in Tibet?" Chavasse said. "Seeing firsthand how well the grateful peasants are responding to the new regime?"

"Something like that." Kurbsky shrugged. "I have what you might describe as a roving commission. I'm a staff writer for *Pravda*, but my work appears in newspapers and magazines all over the Soviet Union."

"I'll bet it does."

"This little adventure will make most interesting reading," Kurbsky continued. "The mysterious Englishman, if that is what you are, landing guns by night disguised as a Tibetan. It's a great pity you couldn't have been an American. That would have made it even more sensational."

The flame of the spirit lamp, flickering in the wind, danced across Kurbsky's face and there was a glint of humour in his eyes. An involuntary smile tugged at the corners of his mouth, and Chavasse sighed. It was hard not to like a man like this.

"What happens now?"

"Some coffee, a little supper and sleep if you can manage it."

"And tomorrow?"

Kurbsky sighed. "Tomorrow we go on to Changu and Colonel Li, the military commander in this area." He leaned forward, and his good-humoured face was solemn. "If you take my advice, I would tell him what he wants to know, without any foolish heroics. They tell me he is a hard man."

For a moment, there was a silence between them, and then Kurbsky slapped his thigh. "And now, some supper."

He made a sign and one of the soldiers brought coffee and a tin of assorted biscuits.

"Don't tell me the army of the People's Republic is going soft on me," Chavasse commented.

Kurbsky shook his head. "My own private stock, I assure you. I always find that a few little luxuries make all the difference on a trip like this in rough country."

Chavasse swallowed some of the coffee. It was good and he grunted his approval. "Taking a leaf out of the old empire-builder's book, eh? Dinner jackets on safari in darkest Africa and all that sort of thing."

"Thank God for the English," Kurbsky said solemnly. "At least they gave the world respectability."

"At any time a most dubious virtue," Chavasse said, and they both laughed.

"How is London these days?" Kurbsky asked.

For a moment Chavasse hesitated, and then he shrugged. After all, why not? "When I left there was a steady drizzle blowing in from the river, bringing with it all the signs of a typical English winter; there wasn't a leaf in sight in Regent's Park, and five nuclear disarmers had chained themselves to the railings outside 10 Downing Street."

Kurbsky sighed. "Only in London! I was there last year, you know. I managed to catch Gielgud in *The Cherry Orchard* one evening. A memorable performance—for an Englishman playing Chekhov, of course. Afterwards we had supper at Hélène Cordet's Saddle Room."

"For a Russian abroad, you certainly visit the right places," Chavasse told him.

Kurbsky shrugged. "It's a necessary function of my work to mix with all classes and to try to see something of every facet of your society. How else are we to understand you?"

"The sentiment does you credit," Chavasse told him. "Although I can't say it's one I've frequently encountered among Russian journalists."

"Then you have obviously been mixing in the wrong circles," Kurbsky said politely.

One of the soldiers brought more coffee. When he had moved back to the fire, Chavasse said, "One thing puzzles me. I thought things were strained between Moscow and Peking. How come the Chinese are letting you run loose in their most closely guarded province?"

"We have our differences from time to time. Nothing more than that."

Chavasse shook his head. "Don't kid yourself. You people like to make cracks about American political immaturity, but at least they had the good sense to realize before the rest of the world who the real enemy of peace was. China's your problem as well as ours. Even Khrushchev's got the brains to see that."

"Politics and religion," Kurbsky sighed, and shook his head. "Even friends quarrel about such matters. I think it is time we turned in."

In spite of the quilted sleeping bag which Kurbsky gave him, Chavasse was cold. His head was splitting and he was again conscious of that slight feeling of nausea.

He looked out through the tent flap and concentrated on the flame of the spirit stove, trying to will himself to sleep. One soldier had wrapped himself in a sheepskin rug beside the stove and the other paced up and down on guard, his rubber boots drubbing over the frozen ground.

Chavasse thought about Kurbsky, remembering some of the things the Russian had said and the way laughter had glinted constantly in the grey eyes. A man hard to dislike. In other circumstances, they might even have been friends.

He dozed off and awakened again only an hour later, his teeth chattering and his face beaded with sweat. Kurbsky was kneeling beside him, a cup in one hand.

Chavasse tried to sit up and the Russian pushed him back. "There is nothing to worry about. You have a touch of the mountain sickness, that's all. Swallow this pill. It will help."

Chavasse took the pill with shaking fingers and washed it down with cold coffee from the cup which Kurbsky held to his lips.

He folded his arms inside the sleeping bag to keep them from shaking and managed a smile. "I feel as if I've got malaria."

Kurbsky shook his head. "In the morning, you'll feel much better."

He went outside, leaving Chavasse staring up through the darkness and reflecting that you learned something new every day of your life. The last Russian with whom he'd had any direct physical contact had been an agent of SMERSH just before Khrushchev had disbanded that pleasant organization. It hardly seemed possible that he and Kurbsky had belonged to the same nation.

But there was no real answer—no answer at all—and he closed his eyes. Whatever was in the pill, it was certainly doing the trick. His headache was gone and a delicious warmth was seeping slowly throughout his entire body. He pulled the hood of the sleeping bag around his head and, almost immediately, drifted into sleep.

The morning sky was incredibly blue, but the wind was cold and standing by the jeep watching the two soldiers strike camp, Chavasse felt ten years older and drained of all his strength.

Even Kurbsky looked different, his eyes solemn, his face lined with fatigue as if he had slept badly. When they were ready, he turned to Chavasse almost apologetically and made a slight gesture towards the jeep. Chavasse climbed into the rear and sat on one of the spare seats under the swivel gun.

The rolling steppes stretched before them, the short golden grass beaded with frost as the wheels drummed over the frozen ground.

Within half an hour, they came to the great highway which the Chinese had built in 1957 to facilitate troop movements from Sinkiang to Yarkand when they had been faced with an uprising among the Khambas.

"Something of an achievement, wouldn't you say?" Kurbsky asked.

"Depends on your point of view," Chavasse said. "I wonder how many thousands of Tibetans died building it."

A shadow crossed Kurbsky's face. He barked a quick order in Chinese and the jeep moved forward across the steppes, leaving the road, desolate and somehow alien, behind them.

He seemed disinclined to engage in any further conversation, so Chavasse leaned back in his seat and examined the countryside. To one side of them, the Aksai Chin Plateau lifted into the blue sky; before them, the steppes seemed to roll on forever.

Within half an hour they had come down onto a broad hard-packed plain of sand and gravel,

97

and the driver put his foot down flat against the boards.

The jeep raced across the plain and as the cold wind lashed his face, Chavasse began to feel some spark of life, of real vitality, returning to him. The driver changed down as they came to the end of the plain and slowed to negotiate a gently swelling hill. As they went over the top, Chavasse saw a monastery in the valley beneath them.

The shock was almost physical and as they went down the hill, excitement and hope stirred inside him. He turned to Kurbsky and said casually, "Are you stopping here?"

Kurbsky nodded briefly. "I don't see why not. I'm doing a series on Buddhism and this is one of the few monasteries still functioning in this part of Tibet. A couple of hours won't make much difference."

For one insane moment, Chavasse almost blurted out his thoughts, for this could only be one place—the monastery of Yalung Gompa, according to Joro the centre of resistance for the entire area. It was the last place on earth for a Russian and two Chinese soldiers to be visiting, and yet fate had laid out the path for Kurbsky and there could be no turning back. With something strangely like regret in his heart, Chavasse sat back and waited.

The lamasery consisted of several flat-roofed buildings painted in ochre and built into the side of the valley. The whole place was surrounded by a high wall, and great double gates stood open to the courtyard inside.

Flocks of yaks and small Tibetan horses grazed beneath the walls and the black skin tents of the herdsmen clustered beside a stream.

It was a peaceful scene and smoke from the cooking fires, carried to them on the wind, was pungent in the nostrils, taking Chavasse back by some trick of memory to the campfires of boyhood.

A crowd of fifty or sixty people stood by the gate peering into the courtyard, and suddenly the air was filled with an unearthly, deep booming sound that reverberated between the walls of the valley.

Kurbsky pointed excitedly. "See, there on the highest roof. A monk is blowing a *radong*. They can signal with them for miles, I understand."

The crowd by the gate turned towards them. They were mainly herdsmen, hardly mountaineers in sheepskin *shubas*, some with broad knives in their belts. They looked distinctly unfriendly and the Chinese soldier at the machine gun cocked it quickly and checked the magazine. The jeep slowed as the driver changed gear and the crowd parted to let them through.

For a moment, every other consideration was driven from Chavasse's mind at the sight of the magnificent spectacle which was taking place in the courtyard.

A group of lamas in brilliant traditional costumes were in the middle of enacting some religious ceremony. In their silken robes of blue, red and green and wearing huge masks with hideous demons' faces painted on them, they whirled together in an intricate and deadly pattern, wielding great swords above their heads.

"What luck!" Kurbsky exclaimed excitedly. "I've heard of this ceremony. It's something few travellers ever see. The Downfall of the King of Hell."

He opened his knapsack, took out a camera and started to take photos as fast as he was able. For Chavasse, there was a terrible fascination in sitting there, waiting for something to happen, and suddenly he felt curiously light-headed and there was that faint feeling of nausea again.

The demons spun in ever-faster circles, leaping into the air, their aprons of human bones swinging out until they were parallel to the ground. The music from the conches and the drums became even more frenzied and the soldier at the machine gun leaned negligently forward, his mouth agape with wonder.

And then Chavasse realized that the demons had gradually encircled the jeep, that they were moving closer and closer, tightening the circle every moment, and that the crowd who had stood outside had now moved in through the gate.

Kurbsky and his men had noticed nothing.

Once, the Russian cursed and hastily reloaded the camera, then continued to take pictures as fast as he could.

Chavasse had been keeping an eye on one man who seemed to be leading the others in their dance. His robe was scarlet, his mask scarlet and white with dark horsehair tails.

The sword in his hand spun in a glittering circle of steel as he revolved, and suddenly he was very close. His right arm swung from behind his left shoulder in one terrible, backhanded blow. The soldier at the machine gun staggered against Chavasse, his head half-severed from his body, and toppled over the side.

There was a moment of utter stillness during which the whole world seemed to stop breathing, and then the crowd roared and moved in. Everything seemed to move away from Chavasse as the demon wrenched off his mask and Joro glared up at him, his face cold and hard, the face of a killer.

The driver screamed once as hands reached for him, dragging him from behind the wheel, and Kurbsky stood there, his face frozen with horror, the camera still half-raised. He threw one terrible, agonized glance at Chavasse and then was pulled backwards out of his seat.

For a brief moment, he managed to get to his feet, covered in dust, blood on his face, and then they swarmed over him like a great sea, blotting him from sight.

Chavasse found himself scrambling over the

side down into the crowd, his mouth open in a soundless scream as he tried to claw his way through the living wall towards the Russian.

Faces turned towards him, blind with fury and passion, lips drawn back from decaying teeth. As hands clawed at his clothing, he smashed a fist into someone's mouth and then a searing pain flooded through his head and he plunged into darkness.

7

He opened his eyes slowly. For a moment, his mind was a complete blank, and he struggled up on one elbow, panic moving inside him.

He was lying on a narrow bed in one corner of a dark and windowless room. A flickering butter lamp hung from a chain in the centre and all the gods and devils in the Buddhist pantheon chased each other through the shadows on the ancient tapestries which covered the walls.

Their great demons' faces loomed out of the darkness at him and he closed his eyes for a moment and became aware of a low, monotonous voice. When he opened them again, he realized that a saffron-robed monk in a conical hat was sitting in the shadows a few feet away, beads clicking between his fingers as he prayed.

As Chavasse moved, the old man stopped praying, got to his feet and came forward. He looked incredibly old, his yellow parchment face netted with a thousand wrinkles. Quite suddenly, he smiled and, pulling the tapestry at the end of the bed to one side, went out through a low arch.

Chavasse felt completely rested and his headache had vanished. He flung the sheepskin to one side and swung his legs to the floor. At that moment, the tapestry was pulled back and Joro entered.

The Tibetan was dressed in the brown robe and sheepskin *shuba* he had worn on the plane and there was a smile on his face. The other Joro, the one who had worn the mask of the King of Hell, might never have existed.

"How are you feeling?" he said.

"All things considered, pretty good," Chavasse told him. "I don't know what made me act the way I did. I think I had a touch of fever or something."

"It was the mountain sickness, nothing more. It makes a man do strange things. The abbot gave you something for it while you slept."

"That was a pretty neat trick you pulled out there in the courtyard," Chavasse said.

Joro shrugged. "They had the machine gun so we had to be careful. I'm glad it worked. I had to walk most of the night to get here in time. But I knew they would take you to Changu and this meant that they would have to pass through here."

"What happened to the Russian? Is he dead?"

Joro nodded. "Naturally. To my people, the Russians and the Chinese are simply two sides of the same coin. Here is your Walther. I found it in his pocket."

Chavasse sighed, a feeling of genuine regret running through him. "He was a good man, by any standards."

"Not by mine," Joro told him. "To me this is war and he was the enemy. It is as simple as that. In any case, I couldn't have stopped the people once they got started. I had enough trouble saving you when you got in among them."

"My thanks for that, anyway."

Joro shook his head. "They are not needed. I was simply repaying a debt. It was your quickness which saved me at the lake."

"You've found the arms, I suppose?" Chavasse said. "They were in the rear of the jeep."

Joro nodded. "Some of my men are preparing them for use in the next room. Why not come through. There is a fire there and some tea. Tibetan, I'm afraid, but it's time you got used to it."

He plucked back the tapestry and Chavasse followed him into a much larger room with a low, crudely plastered ceiling and tiny windows set high in the wall. The guns were laid out on a large wooden table and three Tibetan warriors cleaned them expertly.

"They seem to know their stuff," Chavasse commented.

Joro nodded. "They are quick to learn. This is something the Chinese have yet to discover."

A fire of yak dung burned brightly on the large stone hearth and as Chavasse watched, Joro crumbled a handful of brick tea into a cauldron of boiling water and added butter and a pinch of salt.

"You haven't got such a thing as a cigarette, have you?" Chavasse asked.

Joro nodded across to the table. "One of my men emptied the Russian's pockets. His things are over there. There were three of four packets of cigarettes, I believe."

Chavasse crossed to the table and stood looking down for a moment at all that remained of a man: a wallet, his travelling papers and three packets of cigarettes.

He lit one slowly and, carrying the wallet and travelling papers, returned to the fire, where he sat down on a rough wooden bench.

The wallet contained a wad of Chinese banknotes, a couple of letters obviously received from friends in Russia and a membership card for a Moscow press club. There were no intimate little snapshots of wife or children, and feeling curiously relieved, Chavasse turned to the papers.

There were the usual travelling permits plus a special visa for Tibet, date-stamped Peking and countersigned by the military governor in Lhasa. They were smeared with blood and badly damaged by a knife-thrust, but Kurbsky's face still stared out from the photo of identification.

Chavasse sat there looking at the papers, so deeply immersed in thought that when Joro pronounced the tea ready and handed him a metal cup, he drank the contents down without thinking.

"The tea." Joro smiled. "You like it?"

Chavasse looked at the empty cup in his hands with a slight frown and then grinned. "I didn't even feel it go down. You'd better give me another."

It was curiously refreshing and he felt life returning to him. He lit another cigarette and said, "How far is Changu from here?"

"Perhaps ninety miles," Joro said. "Two days' hard travelling by horse."

"What if we went in the jeep?"

"That would be impossible," Joro said. "There are at least two hundred troops stationed there, and they patrol the vicinity regularly. If we even tried to approach the town in the jeep, we would be arrested."

"But what if we drove right in?"

Joro frowned in bewilderment. "How would this be possible?"

"By my telling the authorities that I'm Andrei

Sergeievich Kurbsky, a Russian journalist touring Tibet on a visa from the Central Committee in Peking. I speak excellent Russian, by the way."

"And what about your escort?"

"Murdered by the bandits who ambushed our camp during the night. You can be the guide I hired in Lhasa who pretended to fall in with them and saved my life by persuading them to hold me for ransom."

Joro nodded slowly. "I see—and presumably we escaped in the jeep while the others slept?"

Chavasse grinned. "You're catching on fine."

The Tibetan shook his head. "There is one thing you are forgetting. The Russian's papers— they carry his picture."

Chavasse tossed them into the fire. The blood-stained documents started to go brown and curled at the edges. For a brief moment, Kurbsky stared out at him for the last time. Then they dissolved in a puff of flame.

"Let's say the bandits emptied my pockets," Chavasse said. "Anything else?"

Joro shook his head. "Only that it will be very dangerous. There is possibly one thing in our favour. One of my men arrived from Changu last night. Apparently, Colonel Li is away for a few days visiting the outlying villages. Only a captain called Tsen is in charge, and he is young and inexperienced."

"Couldn't be better," Chavasse said. "Even if he radios Lhasa, what can they do except regret such unpleasantness befalling a Russian national in their territory and confirm my existence."

"Assuming that Tsen accepts us, what then?"

"Kurbsky was looking for stories," Chavasse said. "I don't see why he couldn't have visited Changu with the intention of interviewing Doctor Hoffner."

The Tibetan smiled suddenly and his eyes sparkled. "This would really be a very good joke at the expense of the Chinese. Perhaps Doctor Hoffner would even agree to accommodate you at his home during your stay." His smile suddenly disappeared and he looked serious again. "But whatever we do, it must be handled quickly and before Colonel Li returns. He is not an easy man to fool, I assure you."

"Then we'd better get started."

He left Joro to make arrangements with his lieutenants, went outside and stood at the top of a flight of stone steps gazing down into the dusty courtyard.

It was peaceful and deserted except for the row of monks sitting against a wall in the pale sunlight and praying together, their voices only a murmur on the quiet air.

That death had visited this place such a short time before seemed incredible and yet, as he crossed to the jeep, he passed great purple patches of blood which had soaked into the dust.

He climbed behind the wheel and lit a cigarette and thought about life. Five thousand years before, an Old Testament prophet had put it as perfectly as anyone ever could: *Time and chance happeneth to all men!*

For Kurbsky, who had seen so much of danger in his life, death had erupted out of nowhere in this dusty courtyard a thousand miles from nowhere when he had least expected it.

Chavasse shivered involuntarily. It was a sobering thought, and he was still considering it when Joro joined him a few minutes later. Then they drove out through the gates and started their journey.

For the first couple of hours, they followed the winding course of an ancient caravan trail through the steppes, now rutted by the wheels of Chinese military vehicles.

On several occasions they passed herdsmen and their flocks and once, a long caravan of heavily laden yaks and mules. The landscape was harsh and forbidding, with the skyline broken here and there by strange stone shrines and poles bearing sacred garlands and prayer flags.

Almost four hours after leaving Yalung Gompa, Chavasse braked to a halt and touched Joro, who was dozing in the corner, on the shoulder.

Changu stood beside a river in a wide and shallow valley and its flat-roofed buildings climbed the opposite slope in tiers. The most imposing structure by far was the monastery, which stood in the very centre of the ancient walled town, its walls striped in red, green and black.

"Is the monastery still functioning?" Chavasse asked Joro as he engaged a low gear and took the jeep down the steep slope.

The Tibetan shook his head. "Colonel Li uses it as his headquarters. There are only a few monasteries left in Tibet now. Only Yalung Gompa's isolation has saved it so far."

The familiar tents of the herdsmen clustered around the walls of the town and they passed a caravan, causing heads to turn cautiously, and went in through the great archway of the main gate.

Just inside, a white concrete pillbox looked somehow incongruous and three soldiers in quilted drab uniforms squatted in the dust and gambled with dice.

"It's easy to see that Colonel Li is away," Joro said.

Chavasse didn't even bother to stop. As the soldiers glanced up in alarm, he roared forward, scattering men and animals, drove into the courtyard of the monastery and braked to a halt in what he hoped was a suitably arrogant manner.

A soldier lolling against the wall beside the main gate straightened at once and unslung his automatic rifle.

"Shall I come with you?" Joro asked.

Chavasse shook his head. "No, you stay here. It should give you some sort of chance if things go sour on me."

He mounted the broad flight of shallow steps

leading to the entrance, lighting one of Kurbsky's cigarettes as he did so.

The guard stepped forward, fingering his rifle, and Chavasse snapped in Chinese, "Take me to Colonel Li at once, and be quick about it!"

There was just the right amount of iron in his voice and the soldier was properly impressed. He explained hastily that the colonel was away but that Captain Tsen was in his office and he would take Chavasse to him.

They went along a stone-flagged corridor, mounted some stairs at the end and passed into another corridor with a wooden floor. At the far end, the sentry opened a door and stood back respectfully for Chavasse to enter first.

An earnest and rather scholarly-looking young corporal looked up in surprise from his desk. When he saw Chavasse, his eyes widened behind the thick lenses of his steel spectacles and he got to his feet hastily.

"Where's Captain Tsen?" Chavasse demanded angrily.

The corporal opened his mouth to speak, shut it again and turned instinctively to the door behind him. Chavasse brushed past him, opened it and went inside.

The young officer who sat behind the desk was perhaps twenty-five and when he rose to his feet, a frown of bewilderment on his face, Chavasse saw that he was no more than five feet.

"Are you Tsen?" he snarled. "My God, what

sort of a bloody post are you running here? Guards dicing at the main gate and sentries propping up the wall while rebels gallop around at will, murdering your own men."

Tsen tried to assert his authority. He came from behind his desk, fastening his collar, and said angrily to the corporal who stood in the doorway, "What is going on here? Who is this man?"

"Who am I?" Chavasse interrupted. "I'm Kurbsky. Surely they radioed you from Lhasa to say I was coming?"

"Kurbsky?" Tsen said blankly. "Lhasa?"

"I'm a journalist, you dolt," Chavasse roared, "on a roving commission in Tibet to find stories for my paper in Moscow. And a fine story I've got for them, I can tell you. Held prisoner by a gang of murderous cutthroats, my escort murdered. That's going to look good in *Pravda*. I don't know who's supposed to be in charge here, but when the Central Committee in Peking hears about it, heads will roll, I promise you."

Captain Tsen's face was ashen and he pulled a chair forward quickly. "Please sit down. I'd no idea."

"I bet you hadn't," Chavasse said. "I trust you've at least got a drink handy."

Tsen turned to the corporal, who went to a cupboard and returned with a dark bottle and a glass, which he hastily filled.

"What the hell is this supposed to be?"

Chavasse demanded as the liquor burned its way down his throat. "Petrol?"

Tsen managed a smile with some difficulty and went back to his chair. "If I could see your papers, Comrade Kurbsky."

"Papers?" Chavasse said in amazement. "Good God, man, they stripped me of everything. I'm lucky to be here in one piece. Get on the radio to Lhasa—they'll tell you all about me."

Captain Tsen smiled placatingly. "Of course, comrade, but I can attend to that later. Perhaps if you could give me an account of what happened?"

Chavasse ran quickly through his story and when he had finished, Tsen said, "This Tibetan who saved you—he is with you now?"

Chavasse nodded. "He's outside in the jeep, but don't go trying to make him into a hero. He's only helped me because he knew which side his bread was buttered on. They're all damned rogues, these Tibetans. There's only one way you'll solve your problem here, Captain, and that's to stamp on their necks, and stamp hard!"

"How I agree with you, comrade," Captain Tsen said feelingly, "but the Central Committee in Peking has ordained other methods for the time being."

"Then more fools they." Chavasse got to his feet. "If you've no more questions for the moment, I'd like to make a move. I could do with a hot bath and some decent food."

Captain Tsen looked bewildered. "But where do you intend to go? I shall naturally have quarters provided for you here."

Chavasse allowed himself to thaw a little. "That's very kind of you, Captain, but I've been hoping that Hoffner would put me up. After all, he's the man I've come to see."

A great light dawned for Tsen and he jumped to his feet, his face wreathed in smiles. "Ah, but I see now! You have come to Changu to do an article on the good doctor for your newspaper?"

"I can't think of anything else that would have brought me here," Chavasse told him. "I heard about Doctor Hoffner in Lhasa and he seemed to me to be a most extraordinary man."

"But he is. He is indeed, comrade," Tsen said. "The peasants worship him, and this helps our cause enormously." He reached for his cap. "I will conduct you to his house personally."

Chavasse found himself frowning. "The good doctor approves of your work here then?"

Tsen nodded. "But of course. He is a great humanitarian. He and the colonel are close friends. They play chess together."

They paused in the office and he spoke rapidly to the corporal, who grabbed his cap and ran at once from the room. "I have sent him on ahead to warn Comrade Stranoff that we are coming."

"Stranoff?" Chavasse said with a frown as they went downstairs.

"Doctor Hoffner's housekeeper," Captain Tsen

explained. "Her father was Russian, her mother Chinese. A wonderful woman."

There was a sudden warmth in his voice and Chavasse stifled a smile. "I shall look forward to meeting her."

He managed the briefest of nods to Joro as the Tibetan climbed into one of the rear seats to make room for Tsen and they drove out of the courtyard and through the narrow streets.

They passed through the bazaar, where merchants sat with their carpets and bootmakers and silversmiths worked in the open at their trade. People scattered hurriedly as Chavasse sounded his horn, and sullen, unfriendly glances were directed towards them.

Hoffner's house was one of the largest in town. It was a three-storeyed, flat-roofed building surrounded by a high wall, and Chavasse drove through the gate at Tsen's direction and braked to a halt in the courtyard.

He switched off the engine, climbed from behind the wheel and started up the steps to the front porch, Tsen just behind him. At that moment, the door opened and a young, slightly built woman stepped out to greet him.

She wore narrow quilted pants and a Russian-style shirt in black silk edged with silver, buttoned high about her neck. Her hair was quite fair, but her skin had that creamy look peculiar to Eurasian women, her lips an extra fullness that gave her a faintly sensual air.

She had the breathtaking beauty that one always associates with simplicity and Chavasse shivered suddenly and for no accountable reason, as if somewhere, someone had walked over his grave.

She stood before him looking steadily and gravely into his face and then she smiled and it was as if a lamp had been lit within her.

"It is good to see you here," she said in Russian.

Chavasse moistened dry lips. "I am glad to be here," he replied, and as she led him into the house, he was surprised to find that he genuinely meant it.

8

The room was obviously one of the best in the house. The walls were covered in painted plaster and sheepskin rugs were scattered across the wooden floor. Most important of all, the bed looked extremely comfortable.

Immersed in hot water up to his neck, Chavasse leaned back in the large wooden tub by the open fireplace, smoked one of his Russian cigarettes and thought about Katya Stranoff.

She was certainly one hell of a woman, but he was going to have to tread carefully. It seemed quite evident that she was pleased to see him, mainly because the Russian element in her nature was uppermost and she considered herself to be a Westerner, an alien in a strange land.

He wondered how she managed for suitable

male companionship. Heaven knows, Hoffner was too old for her, but Captain Tsen had made no secret of his regard, and there was always Colonel Li, an unknown quantity in more ways than one.

The door opened and Joro entered, carrying a neat bundle which he placed on a chair. He squatted beside the tub and grinned. "The woman told me to bring you fresh clothing."

"I was wondering when you'd show up," Chavasse said. "Are they treating you all right?"

Joro nodded. "I'm sleeping in the kitchen, which is warmer than the stables at least." He frowned and shook his head. "There have been changes since I was last here."

Chavasse reached for a towel, stood up and started to dry himself roughly. "In what way?"

"There's no longer anyone here I know, which in some ways is a good thing, and I'd never met the Stranoff woman before today. There are only two servants now, a man and his wife."

"And why should that worry you?"

"Because they're both Chinese and they don't care for Tibetans—they've made that plain enough already."

"And you think they're working for Colonel Li?"

Joro nodded. "One can't be certain, but I think you'll have to be very careful."

"Don't worry," Chavasse said with feeling. "I intend to be."

He dressed quickly in the clothes which Katya Stranoff had sent up. There was a black silk Russian shirt like the one she had been wearing, a pair of quilted pants and a heavy woollen sweater.

He examined himself carefully in the mirror, combed back his hair and turned to Joro. "How do I look?"

Joro grinned. "Very pretty. I'm sure she'll be impressed."

"Let's hope so," Chavasse told him. "It might prove to be important. You'd better go back to the kitchen now. I'll see you later."

As Chavasse was going downstairs, a door clicked open and Katya Stranoff crossed the hall. She paused as she heard his foot on the stairs and glanced up, and her eyes sparkled in the lamp light.

She was wearing a Chinese sheath dress of heavy black silk embroidered with scarlet poppies, which fitted her lithe body like a second skin. It buttoned high about her neck, and two discreet vents on each side of the skirt gave him a glimpse of slender legs as she moved to greet him.

"You certainly look better for the bath. All you need now is a drink and a decent meal."

"I'd love both," he said, "but first, would it be in order for me to compliment you on that astonishing dress?"

He could have sworn that she blushed, but in

the lamplight it was difficult to be sure. She took his arm and smiled. "Doctor Hoffner is waiting to meet you."

She opened the door and led the way into a large and comfortable room. The walls were shelved from ceiling to floor and packed with books, and a table in the centre was laid for a meal. A pleasant fire burned on the large open hearth and flames danced on the shiny surface of a grand piano which stood against one wall by the window. The whole room possessed a wonderful air of peace and tranquillity.

The man who had been sitting reading in a chair by the fire turned and got to his feet. Wearing an old corduroy jacket and an open-neck shirt, he was one of the largest men Chavasse had ever seen, with a great breadth of shoulder and hair like a snow white mane swept back behind his ears. But it was the remarkable eyes which most impressed Chavasse. They were dark and deep and full of a tremendous serenity.

For a brief moment they registered puzzlement and there was a slight frown, and then Hoffner smiled and held out his hand. "This is a great pleasure, Comrade Kurbsky. A very great pleasure. We don't often see visitors in Changu."

"I've looked forward to this meeting for some time," Chavasse said. "May I compliment you on the excellence of your Russian?"

"You must praise Katya for that, not me." Hoffner glanced at her affectionately. "When she first came here a year ago, I knew no Russian at all."

She kissed his cheek. "Come and eat. Comrade Kurbsky must be hungry. Afterwards, there will be time to talk."

She had obviously gone to considerable trouble to make the meal into something of an occasion. There were candles burning on the table and the food was surprisingly good. They had a clear chicken soup, mutton, boiled rice and chopped vegetables, Chinese style, and the dessert was tinned pears. There was even a bottle of very passable wine.

As he rose from the table, Hoffner sighed and shook his head. "I don't know how she does it, Kurbsky. I really don't."

"What a hypocrite he is," Katya said to Chavasse. "Each week he allows poor Colonel Li to win one game of chess, which puts him in such a good mood that he willingly gives me anything I ask for."

"Colonel Li is one of the finest chess players I've ever known," Hoffner said. "He needs no assistance from me when it comes to winning. But I must say he's very good to us."

They went and sat by the fire, and Katya made coffee over a small spirit lamp. She looked very attractive with the firelight gleaming in her fair hair, and Chavasse suddenly felt relaxed and completely at ease.

He lit one of his Russian cigarettes and as he

blew out a long plume of smoke, Katya wrinkled her nose and sighed. "That smell. There's nothing quite like it. It reminds me of home more vividly than anything else ever could."

"Would you care for one?"

She shook her head. "I'd better not. What would I do when you've gone?" She poured coffee into delicate porcelain cups and handed him one. "How is Moscow these days?"

He shrugged. "There's a lot of new building going on in the suburbs, but otherwise just the same. To tell you the truth, I see very little of the old town. I spend most of my time abroad."

"A foreign correspondent's life must be very interesting," he said. "Always new places, new faces."

"It has its moments. Unfortunately, I never seem to stay anywhere long enough to really get to know the place."

"What brought you to Tibet exactly?"

He shrugged. "There's a lot of interest in Russia about what's going on here. Besides, a good newspaperman goes where there's news and the prospect of a worthwhile story."

"And have you found one?"

"My experience of yesterday will do for a start," he said. "But I'm really hoping to get something out of the doctor here."

Hoffner, who had been listening to their conversation as he lit his pipe, raised his eyebrows. "I'm surprised anyone is still interested in me."

"You're too modest," Katya said, and turned to Chavasse. "Seventy-four and he still supervises his clinic every day. Did they tell you *that* in Lhasa? He's given his whole life to this country, and he could have had a professor's chair in my university in Europe at any time he wanted."

"Come now, my dear," Hoffner said. "You mustn't try to make me into some sort of plaster saint. I'm anything but that."

"But that's the way some people see you," Chavasse said. "As a great missionary."

Hoffner sighed. "I'm afraid I gave up that side of my activities years ago."

"May I ask why?" Chavasse said.

"It's quite simple really." Hoffner leaned forward and gazed into the heart of the fire. "I came here as a medical missionary. I wanted to save souls as well as lives. But I found myself amongst a people already deeply religious, who believed in the way of gentleness to an extent almost incomprehensible to the Western mind. What could I offer these people spiritually?"

"I see your point," Chavasse said. "What was the solution?"

"To give them medical aid when they needed it," Hoffner said. "Apart from that, to try to understand them and to be their friend."

"Forgive me for asking a question which might possibly embarrass you, but I'd like to get as complete a picture as possible. Have the Chinese interfered with your work in any way?"

"As a matter of fact they've encouraged me wonderfully," Hoffner said. "My clinic is more crowded than ever. Mind you, I'm not allowed outside the city walls, but that's only for my own protection. The country's still in rather an unsettled state, as you've found out for yourself."

"You would say then that any change of government has been for the better?"

"Most decidedly. Take medical supplies, for example. In the old days, everything I needed had to come in from India by caravan."

"And now?"

"Colonel Li gets me what I want with no difficulty. You know, before the Chinese came this country was still medieval, its people backward and ignorant. All that is changing now."

Chavasse kept a smile on his face, but inside he was worried, because the old man sounded as if he really meant it. Before he could continue the conversation, Katya stood up and smiled. "If you'll excuse me, I'll leave you to get on with your talk. I must visit the kitchen."

The door closed behind her and Chavasse said, "A remarkable young woman."

Hoffner nodded. "Her father was a Russian archaeologist. He was working for the Chinese government in Peking in charge of the excavations at the old Imperial Palace. He was given permission to visit Lhasa before returning home, but died on the way there. Katya came through here with the caravan a week after burying him."

"And she decided to stay?"

"Colonel Li could have made arrangements to send her through to Yarkand," Hoffner told him, "but then I was taken ill with serious heart trouble. For six months, she nursed me back to health. Since then, the question of her leaving has simply never arisen."

"This all makes most interesting material," Chavasse said. "On the whole, then, you would say that you lead a contented life?"

"Certainly!" Hoffner waved his hand round the room. "I have my books and my piano, and there's always the clinic."

"The piano interests me particularly," Chavasse said. "Rather an unusual item to find in so isolated a region. I've been told that your playing is quite remarkable."

"I wouldn't say that," Hoffner said, "but it would be a great blow to me if I ever had to do without music. I had this piano carried in by caravan from India before the war. The lamplight flatters its appearance, mind you, but the tone is still quite good."

He moved across to the piano, lifted the lid and sat down. He played a few chords, a snatch of a Chopin polonaise, and looked up. "Is there anything you would particularly like to hear?"

Chavasse was still standing at the fire, taking his time in lighting another cigarette. He blew out a long tracer of smoke and said casually in English, "Oh I don't know. What about some music suitable for a May evening in Cambridge?"

Every wrinkle seemed to disappear from the old man's face, and for a moment, it was so quiet that Chavasse could hear the wind whispering against the wooden shutters outside the window.

"I knew there was something wrong about you," Hoffner said calmly, also in English. "From the first moment you stepped into this room, I knew."

"You sent a letter to an old friend some time ago," Chavasse said. "You might say I'm his answer."

"So Joro got out?" Hoffner said.

Chavasse nodded. "He's downstairs in the kitchen now. He's the Tibetan who's supposed to have saved my life from the bandits. You can see him later if you like."

"You said something about music for a May evening in Cambridge?" Hoffner said.

Chavasse nodded. "A long time ago, you lost a bet to Edwin Craig, and he and the girl who'd chosen him instead of you sat in a quiet garden on a May evening while you played for them in the house."

Hoffner sighed. "Sometimes I think it was a thousand years ago, and yet I can still smell the fragrance of the lilac, wet after the rain. I can even remember what I played."

He started to play the opening chords of *Clair de Lune* and Chavasse shook his head. "I don't think so, doctor. It was the *Moonlight Sonata*."

For a long moment, Hoffner sat there looking at him searchingly, and then a slow smile spread across his face. He rose to his feet and took Chavasse by the hand. "My dear boy, I wonder if you could possibly imagine just how delighted I am to see you."

They crossed to the fire and sat down. Hoffner pulled his chair forward and they put their heads together. "Tell me, how is my old friend Edwin Craig?"

"In excellent health," Chavasse said, "and very anxious to see you. That's why I'm here."

"To see me?" Hoffner said, and a look of incredulity appeared on his face. "But that is impossible. For one thing, the Chinese would never let me go."

"Never mind about that for the moment," Chavasse said. "If it could be managed, would you be willing to try? I rather got the impression from our earlier conversation that you approved of what's been happening around here."

Hoffner chuckled. "What on earth would you have expected me to say to a foreign correspondent of *Pravda*? Oh, Colonel Li has shown me a great deal of personal kindness, I can't deny that, and he really *has* done everything possible to ensure that I receive all the drugs and medical supplies I need for the clinic."

"I must say he seems remarkably philanthropic for a case-hardened Communist," Chavasse said.

"It's quite simple." Hoffner smiled gently. "I

129

have succeeded in building up a certain standing in this country over the years, and the people have come to trust me. The reason that my clinic has not been closed down is that the Communists believe I not only approve of them, but that I am willing to cooperate with them."

"And the only way to refute this would be to refuse to work at the clinic, which would mean no medical centre for the Tibetans," Chavasse said. "Colonel Li certainly knows how to put people into a cleft stick."

"A facility he seems to share with most good Communists," Hoffner said.

"Which brings me back to my first question," Chavasse told him. "If I could get you out, would you be willing to leave?"

Hoffner tapped ash from his pipe into the hearth and then started to refill it from an old leather pouch, a slight frown on his face.

After a while, he said, "Young man, I am seventy-four years of age. I'm also in rather poor health, which is no good augury for the future. I may not approve of the Communist regime as practised in this country, but they do at least allow me to continue to give medical treatment to a rather backward people who would otherwise have to manage without it. It would seem to me that my duty lies in continuing to offer it to them for the few years that remain to me."

"And what if I said you were needed on the

outside more?" Chavasse said. "A great deal more?"

"I think it would help if you were to explain," Hoffner told him, and smiled suddenly. "It would also help if I knew your real name."

Chavasse shrugged. "It won't mean anything to you, but I don't see why not. It's Chavasse, Paul Chavasse."

"Ah, French," Hoffner said. "How interesting, but I hope you don't mind if we continue to use English for the moment. It makes a delightful change, I assure you."

Chavasse lit a cigarette and leaned forward. "Many years ago you prepared a thesis for your doctorate in mathematics in which you proved theoretically that energy is space locked up in a certain pattern."

Hoffner frowned. "But how did you know this?"

"You mentioned it to Craig in your letter. You also went on to say that you've now carried things a stage further—you've now proved that space itself can be changed into an energy field."

"But I don't understand," Hoffner said in surprise. "Why is Edwin Craig so concerned about what, at best, is an interesting new mathematical concept? All entirely theoretical, I assure you."

"It was, until the Russians sent a man called Gagarin into space to orbit the world," Chavasse told him. "And then sent another to prove it was no fluke."

Hoffner had been in the act of applying a lighted taper to the bowl of his pipe. He paused, and something glowed deep in his dark eyes. "It would be stupid of me to imagine that you are joking?"

Chavasse nodded. "The Americans have already emulated the performance. They're trailing slightly, but catching up fast. I wouldn't like to say who'll be first on the moon. One thing I *am* sure of. It won't be the Chinese. They aren't even in the race."

"Which explains why here in Changu we have been kept in the dark." Hoffner jumped to his feet and paced restlessly across to the window and turned. "For once in my life I feel really angry. Not only as a scientist, but as a human being. To think that while here one day has followed the next like any other, outside, in the world, man has already taken the first steps on the greatest adventure ever known."

He came back to his chair and sat down. His face had become animated and flushed and there was a sparkle in his eyes. "Tell me about it," he demanded. "Everything you know. What kind of propulsion are they using, for example?"

"Both solid and liquid fuels," Chavasse told him. "Multistage rockets, of course."

Hoffner shook his head. "But this is primitive, my friend. To take a satellite to the edge of space is one thing, but to reach the moon or beyond . . ."

"That's where you come in," Chavasse explained. "The Russians have been working for years on an ionic rocket drive using energy emitted by stars as the motive force. They're years ahead of the West. If they keep that lead, it means eventual world domination by Communism."

"And Craig thinks that my new theory can take that lead away from them?"

Chavasse nodded. "I'm no scientist, but he seems to think that with your discovery, we could produce an energy drive for our rockets from space itself. Is he right?"

Hoffner nodded soberly. "Speeds greater than we have ever dreamed of, something essential if the universe is ever to be fully explored."

There was a moment of silence before Chavasse said quietly, "I know your patients are important to you, but you must see now why it's essential that you return to the outside world."

Hoffner sighed heavily and emptied his pipe. "I do indeed." For a moment longer, he stared into the fire, and then he looked up and smiled. "I don't know how on earth you intend to manage it, young man, but when do we leave?" He frowned suddenly. "And what about Katya? I can't leave her behind."

"Do you really think she'd come?" Chavasse asked in surprise.

Hoffner nodded. "She is anything but a political animal, and she has no ties here or in Russia, no family."

Chavasse sighed. "It could be awkward. Let me think about it, but for God's sake don't tell her a thing. What she doesn't know can't be squeezed out of her. That's always important in an affair like this, in case anything goes wrong. There's no need to rush things. We've got five days before my plane returns. The only real problem will be in finding a way of getting you out of Changu."

He had been subconsciously aware of a slight draught on his right cheek for several moments. He turned and found Katya standing just inside the door, holding a tray on which stood a glass of hot milk.

He wondered how long she'd been standing there and, more important, just how much she had heard, but she gave him no sign. She moved forward, handed the glass of milk to Hoffner and said calmly in Russian, "Time for bed, Doctor. It's been a long day."

Hoffner sighed, took a sip of milk and made a face. "You see, my friend," he told Chavasse. "The wheel has come full circle. Like a schoolboy, I do as I am told."

"I'm sure Comrade Stranoff knows what's best for you," Chavasse said.

She smiled down at him enigmatically. "But of course, Comrade Kurbsky. In everything."

For a moment, there was something strange in her eyes. Only briefly, but it told him what he wanted to know before she turned, crossed to the door and went out again.

9

It was pleasantly warm in the bedroom and someone had obviously made up the fire quite recently. Chavasse placed the oil lamp on the table beside the bed, opened the shutters and stepped out onto a covered balcony which ran the length of the house and overlooked the garden at the rear.

There was no rain, but the wind was moist and he inhaled the freshness of wet earth, and then the tiredness hit him and he went back inside and closed the shutters.

As he started to undress, there was a soft knock at the door and Hoffner came in. He carried an old bathrobe over one arm and, smiling, dropped it across the end of the bed. "I thought you might need one."

There was something in his voice, a slight element of strain, that brought a frown to Chavasse's face. "What's wrong?" he demanded.

Hoffner sighed and sat down on the bed. "I'm afraid Katya knows everything."

Chavasse lit a cigarette calmly. "You'd better tell me about it."

"It's very simple. She heard rather more of the tail end of our conversation than we thought. For one thing, she speaks very good English; for another, she's no fool. She's just been to my room. Wanted to know exactly what was going on and who you really were."

"What did you say?"

Hoffner shrugged. "That I'm a tired old man who wants to go home to die and that friends of mine have sent you in to help me get out."

"And nothing more than that?"

"There didn't seem any point at the moment."

"That was wise," Chavasse told him. "After all, she *is* a Russian citizen. Helping you is one thing, but aiding and abetting in an affair, the success of which can only be to the ultimate harm of her country, presents her with a difficult psychological choice. In any case, as I said before, the less she knows, the less she can give out under pressure."

"You know best," Hoffner said, "but I don't think you need to worry. As I said before, she isn't interested in politics. She isn't even a Party member."

"If anything goes wrong and Chinese intelligence gets their hands on her, she'll end up being anything they want her to be," Chavasse told him grimly.

"I suppose you're right." Hoffner got to his feet. "You'd better have a word with her in the morning; at the moment she is quite convinced I'd be committing suicide. That my heart wouldn't stand the trip."

"I'll handle it," Chavasse told him. "You get some sleep and don't worry. Everything's going to be fine, I promise you."

The door closed softly behind the old man and Chavasse stood there for a moment, thinking about the whole affair, and then the tiredness hit him again, driving everything else from his mind.

He had barely sufficient strength to strip the clothes from his body and climb into bed. He blew out the lamp and, for a while, lay there, allowing each tired muscle to relax, staring up at the shadows on the ceiling, and then he was asleep.

He was not aware of coming awake, only of the fact that he was lying there and that the fire was almost out. He raised his wrist and the luminous dial of his watch glowed through the darkness. It was just after two A.M., which meant that he had been asleep for no more than four hours. And yet he no longer felt tired.

As he lay there, the very air seemed electric

and humming with energy, as if there was nothing sleeping, as if, outside in the darkness, a presence waited for something to happen.

In the distance, thunder rumbled menacingly and then lightning flared, and in the split second of its illumination he saw each item of furniture in the room clearly.

He swung his legs to the floor, reached for the bathrobe Hoffner had provided him and padded across to the window. As he opened the shutters and stepped out onto the balcony, the rain came in a sudden great rush, filling the air with its voice.

It was bitterly cold, but for a moment or two he stood there breathing deeply, taking the freshness into his lungs, filled with a strange inward restlessness.

A quiet voice said in English, "The night air is not good for one at this altitude, Mr. Chavasse."

He turned slowly, every sense alert. Katya Stranoff stood a few feet away by the rail and as lightning exploded again, her face seemed to jump out of the night, the high cheekbones somehow accentuating the depths of her dark eyes, her flaxen hair falling down to her shoulders.

And she was beautiful—that was the thing that came to him suddenly and with a sense of wonder. That she was pretty and attractive had been perfectly clear previously, but in that split second as the lightning had flared, he had seen something more.

There was about her an air of innocence trying desperately to come to grips with the harsh realities of the world, reminding him, with a pang, of another girl in another time and another place.

"Can't you sleep?" he asked.

She shook her head. "One could say I've got too much on my mind."

"Then let's go inside and discuss it," he said. "The fire is almost out in my room, but it's quite warm."

She moved past him without a word and he followed her in and closed the shutters. When he turned, he saw that she had poked the fire into life again and replenished it with a couple of logs from the pile that was neatly stacked at one side of the hearth.

She sat on the sheepskin rug and held her hands to the blaze, and he pulled a chair forward.

"I saw Hoffner leaving your room earlier," she said without looking at him. "I suppose he told you about our conversation?"

He nodded. "You mean about your eavesdropping on us when we were talking after dinner?"

She turned quickly, and something sparked in her eyes. "I'm not ashamed. He's an old man. If I don't worry about him, no one else will."

There was a toughness in her voice, an indication of something stronger in her than he would have imagined, and he grinned and held up a hand in mock alarm. "Hey, I'm on your side."

"I'm sorry," she said, immediately contrite, "but Hoffner's been like a father to me. He's a very wonderful man. I only want what's best for him."

"We're in agreement on that point, for a start."

"But are we?" she asked. "Do you honestly think that a seventy-four-year-old man with a weak heart has the slightest chance of enduring the kind of trip you contemplate?"

"Under the right circumstances, I do," Chavasse told her.

"But he's a sick man," she insisted. "Do you seriously think he could survive a trip on horseback at this altitude over some of the roughest country in the world?"

"Maybe he won't have to."

She frowned at once. "I'm afraid I don't understand."

"You don't have to, and neither does the doctor for the moment. Just leave the details to me." He leaned forward and grinned. "And relax. Everything's going to be fine, I promise you."

She shook her head in exasperation. "You make everything sound so easy—just like my father used to. If he said something, then it had to be."

"It's not a bad way to live."

"You think so?" She sighed. "He said we would go to Lhasa by caravan. That it would be simple, the journey of a lifetime. His plans didn't include dying of typhoid on the way."

"How could they?" Chavasse said gently. "Death has a perverse habit of making his own appointments."

In the short silence which followed, he took out his cigarettes and offered her one. She accepted without a murmur and he gave her a light.

After a moment, she said, "The real Kurbsky—he's dead, isn't he?"

He nodded soberly. "I'm afraid so."

"Did you kill him?"

143

He shook his head. "He and his escort really were ambushed by partisans. They obviously cared as little for Russians as they do for Chinese."

"I see," she said. "And you simply assume his identity? These partisans—were they friends of yours?"

He shrugged. "In a manner of speaking. If you mean could I have saved Kurbsky's life, I'm afraid not. I didn't have that kind of influence with them."

"What about this Tibetan who came here with you? Joro, I think you said his name was. Couldn't he have done something?"

"You obviously haven't been mixing in the right circles," Chavasse told her "As far as these people are concerned, this is war. They're fighting against a brutal invader who's attempting to change this entire way of life by force."

"Please," she said. "I'm not a child. I know that the Chinese have done some terrible things here, but all this bloodshed and killing." She shuddered. "It seems such an appalling waste of human life."

"Perhaps it is," he said, "but remember what Lenin once said: The purpose of terrorism is to terrorize. It's the only way left for a small people to fight back against an empire."

"My father used to say that no man was God," she said, "least of all Lenin. I'm afraid he didn't care for him very much."

"He sounds like a man after my own heart," Chavasse said. "Tell me about him."

She shrugged. "There seems so little to tell now. He was a scholar, you see, with no interest in government or politics. I think that, of all activities, archaeology is the one in which the State can interfere least. We tended to live very much our own lives."

"What about your mother?"

"She died when I was born. I spent my early years at school in Moscow with an aunt of my father's. When I was a little older, he was able to take me with him on his field trips. We lived in Peking for the last three years of his life."

"Why was he so keen to visit Lhasa?"

She shook her head. "I don't really know. A

dream he'd had for a very long time, I think. It seemed like a good opportunity before returning to Russia."

"Don't you ever feel like going back yourself?"

"Not really," she said. "Oh, I miss the theatres, the books, all that sort of thing, but nothing else. My aunt died three years ago, and I've nobody else."

"Except for Hoffner," Chavasse said gently.

She turned, a warm smile illuminating her face. "That's right. Except for Hoffner. He took me in when I was sick and nursed me back to health. He's come to mean a great deal to me."

"He seems to feel exactly the same way about you," Chavasse told her. "Did he tell you he wants you to leave with us?"

She nodded. "I would go with him gladly, I want you to accept that. It's just that the whole affair seems so impossible."

He shook his head. "Believe me, it isn't. I might almost say it's going to be astonishingly simple. But you needn't worry about that for the time being. We've got several days to kill before we can make a move. We're better off here, considering the state of Hoffner's health and his age, than roughing it in the hills."

"I see." She got to her feet. "We'll just have to wait as patiently as we can, I suppose, until you're ready to take us into your confidence?"

She sounded slightly angry, and he stood up and smiled. "Don't take it like that. I'm only

145

thinking of you and the doctor. What you don't know can't harm you."

He placed his hands on her shoulders. "The only real problem's going to be how to pass the time. What do you do for amusement round here?"

She shrugged. "Not very much. I usually go horseback riding outside the walls if the weather's reasonable."

"Now that sounds just my style."

She relaxed suddenly and smiled. "Perhaps you'd like to come with me? I usually go after lunch. How good a horseman are you?"

He grinned. "Pretty fair. Another of my accomplishments."

She nodded. "And you have many, don't you, Mr. Chavasse? It occurs to me that no ordinary man would be able to speak Chinese so excellently and Russian like a native."

"What about you?" he countered. "Your English is pretty good."

She shrugged. "I started to learn it when I was six years of age at my first school in Moscow. It's the standard second language in Russia today." She shook her head. "No, there's still something about you. Something special. Of one thing I'm certain: You're not just an adventurer."

"But I assure you I am," he told her.

She shook her head. "No, there's more to it than that."

And then the thought came to her and her eyes

widened. She took a step towards him, one hand catching hold of the lapel of his bathrobe. "There *is* something more, isn't there? Something to do with the doctor?"

He did the only possible thing. His arms slid around her waist and he kissed her.

Her entire body seemed to come alive and she started to tremble. For a little while, he held her, and then she gently pushed him away.

When she looked up, her eyes were dark and troubled and her face was flushed. "I think I'd better go."

He couldn't think of anything to say as he opened the shutters and she brushed past him. Outside, it was still raining. She turned and looked at him for a moment and suddenly reached up and touched his face with one hand, and then she was gone.

For a little while longer he remained there, his skin crawling with excitement, a small restless wind touching his naked flesh, and then he closed the shutters and went to bed.

10

The day was exhilarating, like new wine, and the blue sky dipped away to the horizon as they rode out through the main gates of Changu shortly after noon the following day.

They were mounted on small and wiry Tibetan horses and Katya urged her mount into a gallop and took the lead. She wore riding breeches and soft Russian boots and her hat and collar were of black astrakhan.

Chavasse, wearing the Tibetan boots and *shuba* he had arrived in, went after her, scattering a grazing flock of yaks as he and Katya skirted the herdsmen's encampment and rode up out of the valley.

The steppes were saffron yellow, golden in the sunlight, and he reined in beside a dark pool of water at the foot of some tall rocks where wind whispered through the dry grass. A bird cried as it lifted across the slope and a strange, inexplicable sadness fell upon him.

He shivered for no accountable reason and then Katya called to him, her voice carried by the wind from the top of a hill in the distance, and he urged his mount forward and went after her.

There was a fine haze over the land that masked the distances and the wind was as warm as a caress. He reined in on top of the hill and saw a river running through a deep gorge below and Katya standing on the edge of the cliffs.

He cantered down the slope, dismounted and sent his horse to join hers with a smack on the rump. He paused to light a cigarette and as he looked up, she turned and headed his way.

She moved through the dry grass towards him and the sun was behind her and the image blurred at the edges. She looked unreal and ethereal and utterly transitory, as if at any moment she might fly away. But when she spoke, the spell was broken at once.

"Let's sit down, Paul."

They flung themselves on the short grass and, after a while, he closed his eyes and relaxed. It was so pleasant, he thought, so wonderfully pleasant to lie in the sun with the right person and do nothing.

He decided there was a lot to be said for beachcombing. Something tickled his nose and he opened his eyes and caught her gently stroking his face with a blade of grass.

"You know, I haven't done this for years," he said.

"But you should. After all, life is for living."

"You've got a point there," he told her. "The trouble is, I never seem to have the time. Some sort of personality flaw, I suppose."

She chuckled. "I don't believe you. Were you the same way when you were a little boy?"

He wrinkled his brow and narrowed his eyes as he tried to somehow measure the limitless depths of the sky. "I can't really remember. My father was French and my mother was English. He was killed fighting with his regiment at Arras in 1940 when the panzers went through Belgium and France like a knife through butter. My mother and I got out through Dunkirk."

"What happened after you got to England?"

He found himself opening up in a way he hadn't done in years, thinking back into the past, half-remembered events suddenly coming to life again.

By the time he had worked his way through to his two years as a lecturer at Cambridge University, almost an hour had gone by.

He stopped talking, and she frowned down at him. "But I don't understand. You had everything you ever wanted and the prospect of a brilliant academic future, and yet you threw it all away."

"I changed my ideas about living, that's all," he said. "One summer vacation, I helped a friend of mine get a relative out of Czechoslovakia. I found I rather enjoyed the experience."

She sighed and shook her head despairingly as though he were a small boy she had discovered engaging in some foolishness. "So you decided to take this sort of thing up permanently?"

"Oh, now I'm expert at it," he said. "They even called me in to help get the Dalai Lama to India last year."

He was giving away too much of himself, he knew that, but she had a strange effect on him, like that of no other woman he'd known before.

"And what does your mother think about it all?"

Chavasse grinned. "She believes I'm some sort of civil servant, which I am, in a way."

Katya still looked puzzled. "And you honestly like this sort of life? Constantly putting your head on the block, never knowing when the axe might fall?"

"Oh, it isn't quite as bad as that all the time," he said. "Working for the Bureau can mean anything from a job like this to making sure nobody shoots Comrade Khrushchev when he visits London. Don't you approve?"

"It isn't a question of approving or disapproving. It's got nothing to do with politics or government or anything like that. It's just that to me, it seems so wrong to see a fine brain wasted."

He closed his eyes, remembering that someone else had once said the same thing. Katya's voice moved on and then it began to rise and fall and then it was the rushing of the river in the gorge and then the quiet trickle of water over stones.

He awakened suddenly. Above him, clouds turned and wheeled across the sky, hinting at a break in the weather. Katya had gone, and he scrambled to his feet and looked about.

There was no sign of her and a slight twinge of panic sent him running to the edge of the cliff. She was standing on a boulder at the water's edge, throwing stones into the river in an abstracted manner. As his boots crushed across the shingle, she turned towards him.

"You deserted me," he told her. "I wakened to find you gone, like the enchanted Tartar princess in the fairy tale."

She jumped down from the boulder and stumbled and he moved forward quickly and caught her in his arms. "Are you all right?"

"Oh, Paul, I wish it were like a fairy tale," she said. "I wish this were an enchanted day standing still in time and that you and I were together for ever and ever."

There was a depth and poignancy in her voice that brought a sudden lump to his throat. For a moment he gazed down into her eyes, and then he kissed her gently. She melted into him and the earth moved, but suddenly she broke away and stumbled across the shingle to the path.

When he reached the top of the cliffs, she was already mounted and galloping away, and it took him a moment or so to catch his horse.

As he went over the top of the hill, clouds moved cross the sun and a great belt of shadow spilled darkness across the ground.

He saw Katya moving towards it and he urged his horse into a gallop because, for some incomprehensible reason, he felt a desperate urgency to reach her before the shadow did.

When he was still thirty or forty yards away, it enveloped her and he reined in his horse. The shadow passed over him in turn and he felt suddenly chilled as fear touched his heart with ice-cold fingers.

For a little while he sat there listening to the sound of her horse's hooves fade into the distance, and when she disappeared, hidden by a fold in the ground, he urged his horse into a walk and followed her.

When he reached the gate of the house, Joro was waiting for him, his face serious. As Chavasse dismounted and handed him the reins, the Tibetan said, "Captain Tsen's been here asking questions."

"What about?" Chavasse said.

"He's making out a report for Lhasa," Joro told him. "He questioned me for half an hour. I told him we were camped near Rudok when they attacked us. I said they dropped the bodies of the two guards down a hole in the ground."

"Sounds reasonable enough," Chavasse said. "Where is he now?"

"Inside. He was about to leave when the Stranoff woman came back. What happened out there? Did you two quarrel?"

Chavasse shook his head. "We decided to have a race on the way home, but my horse was winded." He took his time in lighting a cigarette and said rapidly, "Everything's going smoothly so far. The doctor is willing to come with us, and so is the woman."

Joro frowned. "Are you sure she can be trusted?"

At that moment, the house door opened and Katya and Captain Tsen moved out onto the steps.

"This would seem to be about as good a time as any to find out," Chavasse said, and walked across the courtyard to meet them.

Katya looked quite calm and completely relaxed and Captain Tsen smiled politely. "I hope you enjoyed your ride, comrade."

"In such charming company, how could I fail to?" Chavasse bowed slightly to Katya. "I'm sorry I was eliminated so early in the race. I'm afraid my mount wasn't up to it."

"We must see if we can find you a better one next time," she said. "I believe Captain Tsen wanted a word with you."

Tsen raised a hand. "But there is really no

hurry. I simply wish to hear your own account of your unhappy experience, comrade. For my report to Lhasa, you understand. As it happens, the good doctor has invited me to dinner this evening. Perhaps we could talk then?"

"A pleasure," Chavasse told him.

The Chinese smiled. "Until this evening, then." He saluted Katya, clicked his heels together like a Prussian and walked away across the courtyard.

"You must excuse me," Katya said. "I have to see the cook about the evening meal."

Her tone was formal, almost cold, and before Chavasse could reply she had turned and vanished into the interior of the house. For a moment he stood there, a slight frown on his face, and then he followed her in.

He found Hoffner in the library sitting in front of a roaring fire with a book on his knee, drinking tea from a delicate porcelain cup.

The old man looked up. "Did you enjoy your ride?"

Chavasse warmed his hands at the fire. "It was pleasant enough, but the countryside round here is dreadfully monotonous. I don't think I could stand it for long."

"Oh, it has its points," Hoffner said. "I suppose you know Tsen's been here?"

Chavasse nodded. "I met him on his way out. He's already had a word with Joro. It's nothing to worry about, only some report he has to send to

Lhasa. He said he'd have a word with me tonight after dinner."

"Katya seemed very subdued when she came in," the old man said tentatively. "I take it you've had a word with her?"

Chavasse sat down in the opposite chair and helped himself to tea. "She's far from happy about the whole thing, but she's willing to go along."

"Presumably you haven't told her the real reason I'm leaving?"

Chavasse shook his head. "There's no need. The reason you've given is a perfectly logical one." He hesitated and then continued. "As a matter of fact, Doctor, if anything ever goes wrong with this business and the Chinese question you, tell them exactly what you've told Katya. That you're an old man in poor health who prefers to end his days in his own country. The beauty of it is that it makes perfect sense. They'd probably accept it without probing any deeper."

The old man smiled faintly and shook his head. "But I have the greatest possible faith in the fact that nothing will go wrong."

At that moment, there was the sound of a vehicle braking to a halt outside. Hoffner frowned and put down his cup. "Now I wonder who that can be."

As Chavasse started to his feet, the door

opened and Katya rushed in. "Colonel Li!" she said quickly in Russian.

Chavasse was aware of the extreme pallor of her face, of the dark eyes suddenly smudged with shadow. He managed one quick smile of confidence as the coldness seeped through him, then picked up his cup of tea.

"What an unexpected pleasure," he said calmly.

There were quick footsteps in the hall and a man paused in the doorway. He was almost as tall as Chavasse, his uniform perfectly tailored to his slim figure, and a khaki greatcoat with a fur collar swung from his shoulders.

He carried a riding crop in his gloved hand and, smiling, touched it to the brim of his fur cap. "My dear Doctor, how very nice to see you."

He spoke in Chinese in a deep, pleasant voice and it was obvious that, like Katya, he had European blood in him. His eyes lifted slightly at the corners, but they were shrewd and kindly in a bronzed, healthy face and the lips below the straight nose were well-formed and full of humour.

"We didn't expect to see you back before the end of the week, Colonel," Hoffner said calmly.

"As the English would say, something came up." Li turned to Katya and lifted one of her hands to his lips. "My dear, you look as charming as usual."

She managed a tight smile. "We've had an unexpected guest since you were here last, Colonel. Allow me to introduce you to Comrade Kurbsky, a foreign correspondent of *Pravda* who is here to interview the doctor."

The colonel turned to face Chavasse, who held out his hand. "An honour, Colonel."

Colonel Li smiled good-naturedly and shook hands. "But I've already had the pleasure of making Comrade Kurbsky's acquaintance," he announced.

There was a moment's complete silence in which the whole world seemed to stop breathing. "I'm afraid I don't understand," Chavasse said carefully.

"But surely you remember, comrade?" Li's mouth curved good-humouredly. "Four nights ago at Rangong? We stayed at the village inn together. Filthy hole, wasn't it?"

Chavasse took a quick step forward, kicked Colonel Li's feet from under him and sent him backwards over Hoffner's chair with a stiff right arm.

As he ran out into the hall, he was already reaching for the Walther. There was no time to think of Hoffner or Katya now. This was a matter of survival and in life, as in war, it was the quick and the unexpected that won the day.

A jeep was parked at the bottom of the steps outside the front door and four soldiers lounged beside it, chatting idly. They glanced up in alarm and he turned to go back inside.

Colonel Li appeared in the hall, an automatic

in one hand. Chavasse raised the Walther and pulled the trigger, and nothing happened. He tried again without success, threw the useless weapon at Li's head and vaulted over the parapet into the courtyard.

He landed badly, losing his balance, and as he got to his feet, there was a sudden pain in his ankle. He gritted his teeth and ran for the gate.

Behind him, boots pounded and he heard Li call loudly, "No shooting!"

He was within a yard of the gate when a foot tripped him and he hurtled to the ground, instinctively putting his hands to his face and rolling away to avoid the swinging kicks. A foot caught him in the side, another grazed his face, and then he was on his feet again, standing with his back to the wall.

He caught one brief glimpse of Katya Stranoff's face as she stood in the entrance with Hoffner, and then the four soldiers started to move in.

One of them carried a long military truncheon and darted forward and swung at Chavasse's head. Chavasse ducked, and as the truncheon dented the wall behind him, he lifted a foot into the man's crotch. The truncheon rattled against the ground as the man collapsed.

The other three soldiers hesitated for a moment and then one of them pulled out his bayonet and started forward cautiously.

Colonel Li was running across the courtyard, and he cried out, "No. I want him alive!"

Chavasse dropped to one knee, snatched up the truncheon and smashed it across the soldier's arm. The bone snapped like a dry twig and the man screamed, the bayonet slipping from his nerveless hand.

As Chavasse started to rise, the other two soldiers came in with a rush. The first one kicked him in the side, lifting him against the wall.

He grabbed for the man's foot and they fell to the ground, rolling over and over. As Chavasse pulled himself on top, Colonel Li, who had arrived at that precise moment, picked up the truncheon and hit him one neat and expert blow across the back of the neck.

11

When they threw him into the cell, Chavasse stumbled over a body and fell against the opposite wall. He crouched on his hands and knees and breathed deeply a couple of times to clear his head. After a while, he felt a little better and turned to examine his surroundings.

The cell was perhaps twenty feet square, its only illumination a small butter lamp which stood in a niche in the wall above his head. In its pale light he saw that the place was crammed with stinking humanity. A few heads turned towards him listlessly to stare vacantly a moment before turning away.

Most of them were Tibetan peasants, their sheepskin *shubas* wrapped closely about them while they slept. In one corner, an old lama, his face wrinkled with age, yellow robes torn and soiled, stared into space, fingers clicking through his beads while he intoned a succession of *Om ma-ni pad-me* hums in a low, monotonous voice.

It was unbelievably cold and rain drifted in a fine spray between the bars of the small window set high in the wall. Chavasse got to his feet, stepped over one poor wretch who huddled in a tattered robe, face beaded with fever, and pulled himself up to look outside.

One adobe wall of the courtyard had crumbled away and he could see down into the town. The wind which howled across the flat rooftops of Changu came from the steppes of Mongolia, bringing winter with it, touching his face with cold fingers. He shivered despite himself, a wave of greyness running through him as if somewhere, someone had walked over his grave.

A door opened on the other side and light flooded out into the courtyard, framing a Chinese soldier in the entrance. He turned and spoke to someone inside. There was a sudden burst of laughter and then the soldier closed the door and ran across the yard, head bent against the rain.

Chavasse dropped down from the window. The man with fever was moaning steadily like some animal in pain, lips drawn back, teeth tightly clenched together. Chavasse picked his way cautiously between the sleeping bodies towards a vacant corner near the door and withdrew hurriedly as the appalling stench of human excrement filled his nostrils.

He returned to his original place and sank down into the sodden straw. A few feet away, a huge Tibetan in tattered robe and conical felt hat crouched against the wall and stared at him unwinkingly, one hand scratching for lice. After a moment, he produced a lump of *tsampa* mixed with butter from somewhere about his person, broke it in two and offered Chavasse half. Chavasse managed a smile and shook his head. The man shrugged and started to chew the *tsampa*.

Chavasse started to turn away, his limbs shaking uncontrollably as the cold ate into them. He folded his arms tightly and closed his eyes, concentrating on what had happened, wondering how the hell he was going to get out of this one. But there was no answer. After a while he drifted into an uneasy sleep.

He was conscious of the sound of the key in the lock and of the door opening, but it was the blow to the face that really brought him awake. A hand gripped him by the front of his jacket, jerking him to his feet, and he was pushed across the cell and out through the door.

Two privates and a sergeant waited for him in the stone-flagged corridor, all dressed alike in quilted drab uniforms, the Red Star of the army of the People's Republic on their peak caps the only splash of colour. The sergeant, a small man, turned away without a word and started along the corridor. Chavasse followed, the two privates bringing up the rear, their automatic rifles at the ready.

They mounted a flight of stone stairs to an upper corridor and halted outside a door. The sergeant knocked, listened for a moment and then led the way in.

The room had obviously once been the living quarters of a person of some importance. The wooden walls were beautifully painted, sheepskin rugs covered the floor and logs burned in the large stone fireplace. The green filing cabinet in one corner and the desk in the centre of the room looked somehow incongruous and out of place.

Colonel Li sat behind the desk, a typewritten report in one hand which he now continued to read. Chavasse stood beside a chair a foot away from the desk, his body sagging with fatigue, and examined himself in the narrow gold-framed mirror which hung on the wall behind Li.

The handsome, aristocratic face was haggard and drawn, the eyes dark pools set too far back in their sockets, and blood trickled sluggishly from a cut in his forehead. As he raised a hand to wipe it away, Colonel Li grunted, dropped the report on his desk and looked up.

An expression of immediate concern appeared in his eyes, and he frowned.

"But my dear chap, what have they been doing to you?" he demanded in impeccable English.

"Your concern is so touching," Chavasse told him.

Li leaned back in his chair, a slight smile tugging at one corner of his mouth. "So, you speak English. You see, already we have made progress."

Chavasse cursed silently. He was tired—more tired than he had been for a long time, and because of that he'd fallen for the oldest trick in the book.

He shrugged. "Your round."

"Naturally!" Li said calmly, and nodded to the sergeant and two privates, who immediately withdrew.

The warmth of the room was beginning to make Chavasse feel a little light-headed. He swayed slightly, groping for the edge of the desk to steady himself. Colonel Li rose to his feet at once. "I think you'd better sit down, my friend."

Chavasse slumped into a chair and Li crossed to a lacquered cabinet in one corner, opened it, took out a bottle and two glasses and returned. He filled the glasses quickly and pushed one across the desk. Chavasse waited for the Chinese to drink first.

Li smiled faintly and emptied his glass. "Drink up, my friend," he said. "I think you will be surprised."

It was the finest Scotch and Chavasse coughed

a little as it caught at the back of his throat. He reached for the bottle and filled his glass again. "I'm glad you approve," Li said.

Chavasse toasted him silently and took it down in one quick swallow. As the liquor flooded through him, he felt better. He leaned back in the chair and said, "All the comforts of home, eh? You guys certainly have it rough working for the proletariat. By the way, you haven't got such a thing as a cigarette, have you? Your boys cleaned me out. From the look of them, I'd say you don't pay them very often."

Colonel Li produced a packet of American cigarettes from his pocket and threw them across the table with a quick flip of his fingers. "You see, I can supply all your requirements."

Chavasse took out a cigarette and leaned across the table for a light. "What's the matter with your own brands?"

Li smiled pleasantly. "But Virginia cigarettes are extremely good. When our time comes, we will undoubtedly take them all for home consumption."

"Careful, comrade," Chavasse warned him. "In Peking they'd call that treason."

Colonel Li smiled and adjusted a cigarette in his elegant jade holder. "But we are not in Peking, my friend. Here, I am in complete control."

The voice was still pleasant, the mood tranquil, but Chavasse was beginning to recognize the technique, and he grudgingly admitted that it was being carried out by an expert.

"What happens now?" he said.

Colonel Li shrugged. "That depends entirely on you, my friend. If you cooperate, things can be made easier for you."

Chavasse was interested. There was still a suggestion that a deal could be made, that much was obvious; but then, it was all part of a familiar pattern. He smiled at the colonel through smoke. "So there's still a chance for me?"

"But of course," Li said. "All you have to do is tell me who you really are and what your mission is here in Changu."

"What happens if I do?" Chavasse said.

Li shrugged. "We can always make use of those who freely admit their errors."

Chavasse laughed harshly and stubbed his cigarette out in the jade ashtray. "If that's the best you can do, I'm not buying."

The Chinese tapped the desk with one elegant hand and said reflectively, "It's a very great pity."

He sounded genuinely sorry, and Chavasse listened to him in a curious, if detached, sort of way. "What is?"

"The fact that we are on opposite sides. I am not a political idealist or fanatic. I'm quite simply a man who has always adjusted himself to the prevailing circumstances."

"I hope it works out for you," Chavasse said, an edge of irony in his voice.

"Oh, but it will, I assure you." Li smiled gently. "You see, *I* have chosen the winning side, make no mistake about that." He adjusted the papers on his desk into a neat pile. "There is still time for you to change your mind."

Chavasse sighed and shook his head. "No thanks, Colonel. Better move into phase two."

Li frowned. "Phase two? I'm afraid I don't understand."

"You really ought to catch up on your reading," Chavasse told him. "To be precise, the latest publication of the Central Committee in Peking. *Interrogation of Political Prisoners and Aliens.* First you're nice, then you're nasty—with due acknowledgement to Comrade Pavlov, of course."

Colonel Li sighed. "You people really have the strangest ideas about us." He pressed a buzzer on the desk and, almost immediately, the door opened and the sergeant entered and stood behind Chavasse.

Chavasse got to his feet wearily. "Now what?"

The colonel shrugged. "It's up to you. I can give you a few hours to think things over. After that . . ." He shrugged, picked up another report and opened it.

The two privates were waiting outside and they trailed behind as Chavasse followed the sergeant along the corridor and down the stone stairs to the basement and turned into another, more brightly lit corridor. Stout wooden doors were ranged along one wall and the sergeant opened one and motioned Chavasse inside.

He found himself in a small stone cell which was no more than six feet square. There was an iron cot against one wall and no window. The door clanged shut behind him and he was immediately engulfed in darkness. The walls and roof dripped with moisture and he groped his way cautiously towards the iron cot. There was no mattress, but in the state he was in, he could have fallen asleep on the floor. He lay down, the rusty springs digging into his back, and stared up into the darkness.

He had a breathing space. Why, he didn't know, but at once he relaxed, the tension draining out of him. He was so tired; his limbs ached and there was a slight, nagging pain in the centre of his forehead. He sighed and closed his eyes, and immediately, the cell was filled with a hideous, frightening clamour.

He scrambled to his feet, every nerve tingling. A large bell was fixed just above the door and it rang continuously while a red light flickered on and off rapidly.

He was standing there looking up, sick to his stomach, knowing what was to come, when the key grated in the lock and the door was thrown open.

The little sergeant stood in the entrance, hands on hips, and smiled gently. Chavasse moved outside. The two privates were waiting, and they escorted him along the corridor. When the sergeant unlocked the door at the far end, a flurry of rain greeted them as they moved out into the night.

The sergeant walked through the darkness towards a truck parked by the guardroom and Chavasse waited in the centre of the courtyard with the two privates, the wind from the steppes like a bayonet in his back.

He wondered wearily what was going to happen next and then twin shafts of light from the truck picked him out of the night.

The sergeant returned, took out the automatic and made a sign to his two men, who withdrew into the darkness. Chavasse waited. For the moment, he and the sergeant seemed to be alone. He slid one foot forward cautiously, his eye on the automatic, and was deluged with ice-cold water from behind.

It hit with the force of a physical blow. He swung round and received another wave full in the face. The two soldiers stood laughing at him, buckets in their hands.

His whole body seemed to be gripped in a great vice which squeezed the air from his lungs as the wind cut through his soaked clothing, burning into his very flesh. He managed one faltering step towards them, his hands coming up, before the sergeant hit him a blow in the kidneys. As he went down, they moved in, boots and fists thudding into his defenceless body.

*　　*　　*

He was conscious of lying there in the centre of the yard, his face pillowed against the wet cobbles. He opened his eyes and the lights from the truck hurt them, and then he heard voices and was lifted from the ground and carried towards the lighted doorway.

It was with no sense of surprise that he found himself outside Colonel Li's office, supported by the two privates. The sergeant knocked at the door, opened it and they went in.

They stood in front of the desk and for the second time that night Chavasse examined himself in the long, gold-framed mirror. He presented an extraordinary sight. Black hair was plastered across his high forehead. One eye was half-closed and the right side of his face was swollen and disfigured by a huge purple bruise. His mouth was smashed and bleeding and the front of his shirt was covered in blood.

Colonel Li looked up at him and sighed. "You are a very stubborn man, my friend, and to what purpose?" The whiskey bottle and glasses were still there, and he filled one and pushed it across the table. The soldiers lowered Chavasse into the chair and the sergeant held the glass to his lips.

Chavasse moaned in pain as the liquor burned into his raw flesh, but after a moment, a warm glow began to spread throughout his entire body and he felt a little better.

"You put on quite a show," he croaked.

Li's face creased in anger. "Do you imagine I enjoy this sort of thing?" he demanded. "Do you think I am a barbarian?" He pressed a buzzer on his desk. "Enough of this childish game of cat and mouse. I know who you are. I know all about you."

The door opened and a young Chinese woman orderly entered with a file, which she placed on his desk. Chavasse noticed in a detached sort of way as she went out that her uniform fitted her like a glove, leather Russian boots setting off trim legs.

"It is all here," Colonel Li said, holding up the file. "I've been in touch with Lhasa and they contacted our intelligence headquarters in Peking at once. Don't you believe me?"

Chavasse shrugged. "That remains to be seen."

Colonel Li flicked open the file and started to read.

"Paul Chavasse, born in Paris 1930, father French, mother English, so has dual nationality. Educated at Sorbonne and Cambridge and Harvard Universities. Ph.D. in modern languages. Lecturer at Cambridge University until 1955. Since then employed as an agent by the Bureau, a secret organization used by the British government in its constant underground war against the free Communist states."

Chavasse was aware of no particular sense of shock that they knew so much. He was not even afraid. His entire body seemed to ache with pain and it was all he could do to keep his eyes open.

"You've certainly got one hell of a vivid imagination," he said.

Colonel Li jumped to his feet angrily. "Why do you make me treat you like this? Is it the way for intelligent people to behave?" He moved round the desk and sat on the edge, a couple of feet away from Chavasse. When he spoke, his voice was gentle, as if he were trying to reason with a stubborn and wilful child. "Tell me what you are doing here, that's all I want to know. Afterwards, you can have a doctor, a meal, a warm bed. Anything you desire."

Everything was slipping away from Chavasse. To keep his eyes open was an effort and Li's face seemed to swell to enormous proportions. He tried to open his mouth, but no sounds would come out.

The colonel moved close. "Tell me what I want to know, Chavasse. That's all you have to do. I will take care of the rest, I promise you."

Chavasse managed to spit in his face once before coloured lights exploded in his head and a great pool of darkness moved in on him.

12

Trudging along in the rain at the end of the column, Chavasse presented an extraordinary picture. His eyes had withdrawn into dark sockets, his hair was filthy and matted and his gaunt body was covered by an ancient and verminous sheepskin *shuba*.

His wrists were tied tightly together in front of him and the other end of the long rope was looped over the pommel of his guard's high wooden saddle.

He was beginning to feel tired. The rain, blown against his face by the high wind, was icy cold and his stomach ached for food. He slowed a little, and immediately his guard tugged sharply on the rope, sending him stumbling forward onto his face.

The man screamed angrily in Chinese and Chavasse got to his feet painfully and started to hobble forward again. "All right, you bastard," he shouted in English. "Keep your bloody hair on."

He could see Colonel Li riding at the front of the column of thirty men, all mounted alike on wiry Tibetan horses, submachine guns across their backs, and he wondered again at the strange mixture of the old and the new that seemed so typical of the Chinese.

Despite the size of the area under his supervision, Colonel Li had only three jeeps and one truck, and when he made his rounds of the villages on the high plateau, where security was bad and he needed a strong escort, he was compelled to use cavalry.

The rain increased in force and Chavasse trudged on, feeling utterly miserable, the coldness seeping into his very bones.

He was perhaps at the lowest point in his life, and he knew that the fact that he admitted this even to himself was extremely dangerous. Colonel Li would have been surprised if he'd known how close he'd been to cracking. He raised his bound hands to wipe rain from his face and stumbled on.

For almost three weeks he had been beaten and humiliated in every conceivable way. Night after night, the bell in his cell had rung and the red light had flashed and sometimes they had come for him and sometimes they had not.

It was all part of a plan. All good sound psychology. Pavlov had started it with his dogs and the bell that sounded at mealtimes, had shown the world that gradually, by changing the order of things, you could produce a complete neurotic breakdown until a man became as broken in spirit as he was in body. Then and only then, the Party believed, could the process of rebirth begin. When the process was finished, the Party had another loyal and efficient zombie to swell its ranks.

He wondered how Katya and Dr. Hoffner were making out. And then there was Joro. Colonel Li had made no reference to the Tibetan since the day Chavasse had been taken.

The rain hammered against his face and he gave up trying to shrug it off and withdrew into his secret and inner self, the one trick that had kept him going for the past twenty two days.

For a moment, he thought longingly of his cell; at least it had been dry and one had food occasionally. And then he shuddered, remembering the night they had come for him eight times and the day Li and Captain Tsen between them had interrogated him for twenty-four hours.

He wondered why Li had decided to take him with him on his tour of inspection—Li, with his phony kindness and fine scholarly face masking the heart of a fiend.

Chavasse tried to imagine how he would kill him if he had the chance. It was a game which had relieved the tedium of many long hours in his cell, but he was too exhausted to think straight and his body was shaking with the cold.

He stumbled and fell again and this time there was no impatient tug on the rope. When he looked up, he saw that the column had halted in the shelter of an outcrop of rock overlooking a valley in which a small village nestled, the smoke from its fires heavy on the rain.

The guard unhooked the rope from his saddle and Chavasse went and sat against a rock, taking advantage of the brief respite, his head resting on his knees.

A stone rattled in front of him and Colonel Li said in English, "But Paul, you really look quite ill. Can I do anything for you?"

He sounded genuinely concerned and Chavasse looked up and said wearily, "Why don't you go fly your kite?"

Colonel Li laughed pleasantly, sat himself on a nearby boulder and poured hot tea into a plastic cup from his flask. He held it forward. "Here, have some."

Chavasse hesitated for a moment and then snatched the cup before Li could change his mind and swallowed the contents.

The tea was red-hot and it burned its way down into his gullet. He leaned over, coughing and choking, and Li patted him on the back. "There now, you'll feel better in a moment."

After a while, Chavasse sat up and handed him the cup. "I'd like to know what's going on behind that smile," he said. "You haven't brought me out here for the good of my health, that's obvious."

"For the good of your soul, Paul," Colonel Li said. "For the good of your immortal soul."

"Communist version, of course."

Li smiled faintly and inserted a cigarette into his jade holder. "You know, I've grown very fond of you during the past three weeks, Paul. I'm really quite determined to bring you over to our side. Such good material going to waste."

"I'll see you in hell first," Chavasse told him.

"I don't think so." Li shook his head. "You seem to forget that I have an irritating habit of always getting what I want in the end."

"I hadn't noticed."

"Oh, but I do. For example, when you first came to me, you refused to tell me who you really were. I found out for myself quite quickly from intelligence records in Peking. Next, I wanted to know what you were doing here."

"You've been trying to find that out for three weeks," Chavasse said, "and how far have you got?"

Li chuckled. "But I've known from the beginning. Katya told me all about it that first night. You were hoping to get Doctor Hoffner out of Tibet."

181

Chavasse moistened dry lips. "Katya told you?" he said dully.

"But of course. It's really very simple. It was quite obvious to me that you had a reason for being at Hoffner's house posing as Kurbsky. I invited the good doctor to tell me all he knew. Being the humanitarian he is, he of course declined. I pointed out that his attitude might have an adverse effect on our future relations. Katya stepped in at once and told me the whole story to save him any possible unpleasantness."

"So now you know," Chavasse said. "I'm glad she had the sense to tell you. What have you done with them?"

"They're both still at Hoffner's house. I'm afraid I'll have to send them to Lhasa eventually and from there to Peking, but only when this affair is cleared up."

"But what else is there to know?" Chavasse asked.

"Many things." Colonel Li shrugged. "How you entered Tibet. Who helped you when you got here, what happened to Kurbsky and his escort."

"You've been asking me those questions for three weeks," Chavasse told him, "and where has it got you? Don't you ever give up?"

"No, Paul, I do not." Li's voice was suddenly ice-cold. "Because in the first place, I'm not entirely a fool. There's something wrong with this affair, something not quite right about it. I want to know what it is."

Chavasse laughed in his face. "You might as well shoot me and get it over with."

"Oh, no, Paul. I won't do that. Before I'm finished with you, you're going to tell me what I want to know—the truth. The whole truth, and you'll tell me because you want to. Afterwards, you'll go to Peking, where I've no doubt the Central Committee will find you a most valuable ally."

"Kill me," Chavasse told him. "You'll save us both a lot of grief."

Colonel Li shook his head. "I'm going to help you, Paul. I'm going to save you in spite of yourself."

He stood up quickly and walked away and, a moment later, mounted his horse at the head of the column. Chavasse waited for his guard and after a while, the man came and looped the end of the rope over the pommel of his saddle again and the column moved off down the slope into the valley.

As they neared the village, dogs ran to meet them, their barking hollow on the damp air. They darted in and out amongst the horses and the soldiers cursed and kicked out at them.

A few ragged and undernourished children hovered on the perimeter of things, keeping pace with the column as it entered the village.

Chavasse decided that he had seldom seen a

more miserable sight in his life than the mud streets and wretched hovels grouped round the large square. He trailed along at the rear of the column, dogs yapping at his heels as the children ran beside him shouting excitedly.

In the centre of the square there was a large stone platform, and here the headman waited with a few elders grouped around him. Colonel Li reined in his horse beside them and waited while his men galloped through the wretched streets, turning the inhabitants out into the rain, herding them into the square.

Within ten minutes their task was done and a crowd of perhaps a hundred and fifty people were gathered in the square. Li made a sign and a soldier pushed Chavasse forward and up onto the stone.

He looked out into the rain over the sea of sullen, apathetic faces, at the cavalrymen lined up at the rear, and wondered what was supposed to happen now.

He soon found out. Colonel Li raised a hand for silence. "People of Sela!" he shouted. "Many times in the past I have told you of the foreign devils who are our enemies. Those of the Western world who would do us harm. Today I bring you such a one that you might look upon him for yourselves."

There was a slight stirring in the crowd, but otherwise not a flicker of interest, and he continued, "I could tell you many bad things about this man. I could say that he has murdered your own countrymen, that he intends you all great harm, but he has been guilty of one single crime more diabolical than all the rest put together."

There was suddenly complete silence as everyone waited and Li said slowly, "This man is one of those who helped kidnap the Dalai Lama—who snatched the living God away by force to India, where he is now held captive against his will."

There was a sudden cry from someone at the back, and then another. In a moment, the whole crowd was surging forward. A stone curved through the air. Chavasse moved to avoid it and another caught him above his right eye, drawing blood.

Filth and ordure of every description snatched up from the mud of the square was thrown at him, and within minutes he was plastered from head to foot.

Colonel Li had wheeled his horse away as they began, but now he called from the edge of the crowd, "What punishment is fit for such a monster?"

For a moment, the crowed paused, and then someone screamed, "Kill him! Kill him!"

Chavasse kicked out in a panic as a hand reached for his feet and fingers grabbed the edge of his tattered robe. Someone caught hold of the rope which was still fastened to his wrists and pulled on it, jerking him headfirst into the crowd.

He was on his face in the mud surrounded by a forest of legs, and fear rose into his throat, choking him, and he screamed and kicked out frantically and then the crowd scattered as the cavalrymen thundered into them.

They cleared a circle and he scrambled to his feet and faced them. The people looked at him silently, hate in their eyes, and Colonel Li urged his horse forward and said, "No, death would be the easy way out, comrades. We must help him to change. To become like us. To think like us. Is this not so?"

There was a sullen murmur from the crowd and, as Li inclined his head, the cavalrymen herded them away.

Li smiled down at Chavasse. "You see, Paul, without me they would have killed you. I really am your friend after all."

Chavasse, glaring up at him with hate in his heart, could think of nothing to say.

13

Lying in the darkness, suspended in a sort of limbo, Chavasse was dragged back into the present when the bell started to jangle somewhere inside his head and the cell was illuminated by intermittent flashes of scarlet.

The skin on his face seemed to tighten, and it seemed as if the raw ends of his nerves were being given a series of electric shocks.

He lay there staring up at the ceiling, the bare springs of the iron cot digging painfully into his back, and waited for them to come for him.

He could hear boots on the flagstones of the corridor and then the key grated in the lock. The bolt was thrown back and a shaft of hard white light sliced through the darkness.

Slowly, very slowly, he swung his legs to the

floor and got to his feet. There was no one but the little sergeant, and he stood back and motioned Chavasse outside with a quick jerk of his head.

Chavasse moved along the corridor through a curtain of grey shimmering cobwebs, dragging his feet slightly. He'd had nothing to eat for three days and, as he put each foot down upon the flagstones, he seemed to be moving in slow motion.

He was filled with a great calm and he turned and smiled at the sergeant as they reached the end of the corridor and started up the stairs. The sergeant looked at him strangely, and there was something that was almost fear in his eyes.

But why should he be afraid of me, Chavasse asked himself? As he paused outside the familiar door and waited for the sergeant to open it for him, he smiled again.

In the outer office, the smart young woman orderly sat at a desk writing busily. She looked up and nodded and the sergeant opened the inner door and stood back for Chavasse to go in first.

Captain Tsen was sitting behind Colonel Li's desk, and he kept his head down as he studied a typewritten report, completely ignoring Chavasse and the sergeant.

Chavasse didn't mind in the least. Through the cobwebs, a gaunt and bearded stranger looked out at him from the mirror on the wall. He smiled and the stranger smiled back and behind the stranger was the sergeant standing by the door and there was that look of fear in his eyes again.

But why should he be afraid? The stranger in the mirror frowned as if he too puzzled over the problem and then a great light flamed through the cobwebs, clearing them instantly. *There was nothing more they could do to him*. That was the only answer. *He had won.*

Captain Tsen looked up, his face completely devoid of expression. He opened his mouth and his voice sounded far away, as if it came from the other end of a tunnel.

Chavasse smiled politely and Tsen picked up a typewritten document and started to read aloud, and now Chavasse heard every word loud and clear.

> *"Paul Chavasse, you have been tried by a special court of the Central Committee of intelligence in Peking and found guilty of grave crimes against the People's Republic."*

There didn't seem much he could say. There was, of course, the small and obvious point that he had not been present at his trial, but such minor items had little significance in the general scheme of things.

He waited and Tsen carried on:

> *"It is the sentence of this court that the prisoner be shot to death as soon as may be convenient."*

It was as if a great floodgate had been released, and joy surged through him in a wave of emotion that brought tears to his eyes.

"Thank you," he said. "Thank you very much."

Tsen frowned up at him. "You are to be executed. You understand?"

"Perfectly!" Chavasse assured him.

Tsen shrugged. "Very well. Take off your clothes."

Slowly, with fumbling fingers, he started to strip, and the stranger in the mirror nodded encouragingly and followed suit. As Chavasse dropped his filthy shirt upon the floor, Tsen said to the sergeant, "Examine his clothing. There must be no question of his evading the sentence by committing suicide."

When Chavasse had finished, he stood in front of the desk, naked as the day he was born, and stared down in wonder at the sergeant, who was kneeling on the floor, examining every article of clothing thoroughly.

Tsen pressed a buzzer on the desk and returned to his report. After a moment, the woman orderly came in. She stood beside the desk, completely ignoring Chavasse, while Tsen spoke to her. She took the papers he gave her, crossed to a large green cabinet and started to file them.

Chavasse stood patiently waiting for the sergeant to finish, and then behind him the door opened and he saw Colonel Li framed in the mirror.

A look of astonishment appeared on Li's face, then was quickly replaced by what seemed to Chavasse to be genuine anger. He crossed the room in two quick strides and hauled Tsen from his seat.

"You stupid swine!" he snarled. "Hasn't he suffered enough? Must he be completely humiliated?"

"But I was simply seeing that he had the customary search before execution, Colonel," Tsen explained. "Central Committee orders are quite explicit and the procedure to be followed is most clearly laid down."

"Get out of my sight!" Colonel Li shouted. "And take that damned woman with you!"

Captain Tsen and the orderly hurriedly withdrew and the sergeant started to help Chavasse into his clothes.

"I'm sorry about that, Paul," Li said. "Truly sorry, believe me."

"It doesn't matter," Chavasse told him. "Nothing matters any longer."

"So Captain Tsen's told you?"

Chavasse nodded. "I've won after all, haven't I?"

There was genuine sorrow on Li's face. "I'd have given anything to see this affair turn out differently, Paul, you know that. But it's no longer my responsibility. You've been sentenced to death by the Central Committee, and there's an end to it."

"It's strange," Chavasse said, "but I feel quite pleased about it. I'm even glad my automatic jammed when it did and I didn't put a bullet in your head. It gives you time to find out for yourself that you're wrong. That all of you are wrong."

Li groaned, got to his feet and crossed to the fire. For a while he stared down into the flames, and then he turned. "If only they'd given me a little more time. Just a few more days. You were close, Paul. Closer than you think."

Chavasse shook his head and said tranquilly, "Oil and water don't mix, Colonel. That's basic chemistry. We're a million miles apart, now and always."

Colonel Li slammed one balled fist into his palm. "But we are right, Paul. Our progress is as inexorable as a law of nature. We will win and you will lose."

"You people never take human beings into account," Chavasse told him, "and they're the most variable factor in the universe. Nothing's certain in this life, not for me or you or anybody."

Colonel Li shrugged. "I can see I'm wasting my time talking to you." He pulled back a shoulder, brought his heels together and held out his hand. "Goodbye, Paul."

Chavasse took the hand mechanically because it didn't seem to matter anymore and then he

192

turned and the sergeant opened the door for him and they went out.

When they reached his cell he halted, but the sergeant pushed him forward and stopped him outside another one at the very end of the corridor. He unlocked the door and pushed Chavasse inside.

It was completely dark and he stood there, arms outstretched in front of him as he edged forward, and then his boot rang against the end of an iron cot and, at that moment, a hard white light was switched on.

The man who lay on the cot was swathed in bloody rags and his hands were crossed on his breast as if he were dead. His eyes were closed and no sound issued from his swollen lips. The face was like wax, the skin so translucent that one would have sworn the bone gleamed through, and yet there was the mark of incredible suffering there.

Chavasse slumped down on the edge of the bed, shaking the man's head from side to side. "Joro!" he said dully. "Joro!" and he gently touched the cold face with the tips of his fingers.

Slowly, incredibly, the eyes opened to stare blankly at him, and then there was a faint stirring of life there. The Tibetan opened his mouth to speak, but no sound would come out and after a while, the head fell back again and the eyes closed.

Nothing seemed real anymore, everything seemed part of some unbelievable nightmare. He sat there beside the Tibetan, staring blankly at the wall, until footsteps approached and the door opened.

There were five of them including the sergeant. Two of them took Joro between them and went first, Chavasse bringing up the rear with the others.

When they opened the door at the end of the corridor, a drift of rain blew in on the wind. Outside in the courtyard, it was cold and miserable, the sky black with threatening clouds, everything tinged with early morning.

Captain Tsen was waiting with a file of six riflemen in the centre of the yard and he stayed there, waiting for the sergeant to handle his end of the business as quickly as possible.

Two wooden posts, about ten feet apart, had been hammered into the ground a yard away from the opposite wall, and Chavasse waited while they roped the unconscious Joro into place.

When they seized him in turn and tied him expertly, he was conscious of no fear. He didn't even feel the bite of the ropes as they were pulled tightly about his arms.

At last they were finished and the soldiers moved away and took up position on one side, the sergeant standing in front of them. Then everybody waited.

Soon Colonel Li appeared at the top of the steps in the main entrance. He was wearing his dress cap and white gloves, everything very formal and correct, and Captain Tsen turned and saluted.

Li came down the steps slowly and crossed the courtyard. He stood a few feet away, hands behind his back, and looked straight at Chavasse, and then he brought his heels together in a quick gesture, saluted and turned away.

Tsen barked a quick order and the six riflemen moved forward quickly and raised their weapons. Chavasse seemed to see everything through the wrong end of a telescope and to hear all sounds as if they were muted and far off. He saw Tsen's mouth open, the arm start to fall, and he closed his eyes.

The volley echoed flatly across the town through the heavy rain and he waited for death, but it did not come.

Somewhere through the quiet that surrounded him he was aware of footsteps approaching him, and he opened his eyes. Joro hung forward, his dead, useless body straining against the ropes that held it to the post, and Colonel Li stood a few feet away, examining it dispassionately.

As Chavasse stared uncomprehendingly at Li and Joro, his frozen mind refusing to accept what had happened, Tsen barked an order and the sergeant and four men doubled forward. As they untied Chavasse, he looked across at what was left of Joro, at the blood dripping from the shattered face to the wet cobbles.

Li moved forward, his face calm and detached. "That's right, Paul," he said. "Take a good look. It's your fault that poor ignorant fool is hanging there. You got him into this, no one else."

As the ropes dropped away from him, Chavasse started to tremble with reaction. "Why?" he croaked. "Why?"

Colonel Li was engaged in fitting a cigarette into his jade holder. He paused long enough to accept a light from the sergeant, blew out a plume of smoke and smiled gently. "But Paul, you surely didn't imagine we had finished with you?"

As a terrible, soundless scream erupted inside him, Chavasse launched himself forward, his fingers reaching for the throat above the high military collar. He never made it. A fist thudded against the back of his neck, a foot tripped him up and he crashed to the cobbles.

14

There was a light that came very close and went away again. It did this several times. Chavasse found it very irritating. His head was spinning and it was an effort to open his eyes.

When he finally awoke, he was lying in a single bed. The room was small and narrow and over everything there was that peculiar and distinctive hospital smell of disinfectant and cleanliness.

The room was in half-shadow and there was a shaded lamp on the locker beside his bed. A young Chinese nurse was reading in the light of the lamp, and as he pushed himself up she put down her book and moved to the door.

"Get the doctor," she told some anonymous person in the corridor, and closed the door again.

Chavasse grinned weakly. "So I'm still in the land of the living? Life's full of surprises."

She put a hand to his brow. It was cool and sweet and he closed his eyes. "Just rest," she said. "You shouldn't even talk."

The door opened and he lifted his eyelids. He saw a brown, kindly face, the skin stretched tightly over high cheekbones and seamed with wrinkles. His wrist was lifted delicately while the doctor looked at his watch and said, "How do you feel?"

"Lousy!" Chavasse told him.

The doctor smiled. "You have an amazing constitution. Most men in your situation would have died by now."

"I wouldn't blame them," Chavasse said. "Not after sampling the way you people treat the human body."

"Please!" The doctor shrugged. "Politics are no concern of mine. You will live, that is the only important thing."

"That's a matter of opinion," Chavasse told him.

There was a discreet tap on the door and the nurse opened it. "Colonel Li is here."

The doctor turned to the door as the colonel entered. "Fifteen minutes please, Colonel," he said. "He needs plenty of sleep." He smiled at Chavasse. "I'll see you in the morning."

He and the nurse left and Li moved out of the shadows and smiled down. He looked lean and fit and his uniform molded to him like a glove. "Hello, Paul," he said. "How do you feel?"

"Like a cigarette," Chavasse said. "Have you got one?"

Li nodded. He pulled a chair forward and sat down and then he took out an elegant case and gave Chavasse a cigarette from it. Chavasse inhaled deeply and sighed with pleasure "That's better."

"And so is this, is it not?" Li asked. "Clean sheets, a comfortable bed, the filth washed from your body."

"But for how long?" Chavasse asked.

Li shrugged. "My dear Paul, that is entirely up to you."

"I thought so," Chavasse said bitterly. "You thought I was going to die, didn't you? That explains the deluxe treatment. The minute I'm on my feet, it's back to my cosy little cell and we begin all over again."

"That's right, Paul," Li said calmly. "We begin all over again. I'd think about that if I were you."

"Oh, I will, I assure you," Chavasse told him.

Li moved to the door and turned. "By the way, you're on the third floor of the monastery and there's a guard on the door. Don't try anything foolish."

"I couldn't even walk to the toilet," Chavasse said.

Li smiled faintly. "Go back to sleep. I'll see you in the morning."

The door closed gently behind him and Chavasse stared up at the ceiling and tried to collect his thoughts. One thing was certain: He'd rather die than start the whole terrifying business all over again. That being so, he obviously had nothing to lose.

He pushed back the bedclothes and swung his feet to the floor. He took a deep breath, stood up and began to walk.

He felt curiously light-headed and for a few moments it was as if he were walking on cotton wool. When he reached the far wall, he rested for a while before turning and walking back.

He sat on the edge of the bed and then tried again. There was a cupboard in the far corner and he opened it hopefully. There was a bathrobe and a pair of felt slippers, nothing else, so he closed the door, padded across to the window and peered cautiously out.

When his eyes became accustomed to the darkness, he saw that the ground was some forty feet below. His heart sank and he turned and went back to bed. He had barely got himself settled again when the door opened and the nurse came in.

She punched his pillows and smoothed the blankets into place. "How do you feel?" she said.

He groaned a little and answered in a weak voice. "Not so good. I think I'll go back to sleep."

She nodded, and there was compassion in her

eyes. "I'll look in later. Try and get some rest."
She left the room as quietly as she had come.

Chavasse smiled softly So far so good, he
thought. He pulled back the bedclothes and
moved across to the door. There was a murmur
of conversation outside and the nurse laughed
and he heard her say, "You'll be bored to death
sitting there all night."

A man's voice replied, "Not if I had something
as pretty as you to keep me company, my flower."

She laughed again. "I'll be round again at half
past eleven to have a look at him. If you're good,
I'll see you get something hot to drink." She
moved away along the corridor and Chavasse
heard a creak as the soldier settled back into his
chair.

He had only one chance—surprise. If he
didn't get away now he knew that he never
would. Tonight was the one slack period. The
time when they thought him so ill and weak that
the very thought of escape was laughable.

He took the bathrobe and slippers from the
cupboard, pulled them on, turned off the bedside
lamp and moved across to the window.

Slightly to the right and about thirty feet
below was the main entrance, where a lantern
swung on an iron bracket, casting a pool of light
down onto the path. A fine rain drifted through
the yellow light like silver mist and he opened
the double-glazed window and leaned out.

Windows stretched to the right and left of

him, yellow fingers of light reaching out into the night through chinks in their shutters. There was no way out above him—the eaves of the roof were several feet out of reach.

A strong wind dashed rain into his face as he leaned far out and looked down. There was no light in the room directly beneath him.

He hardly considered the danger involved as he stripped his bed quickly and knotted two sheets and a blanket together. Underneath the windowsill ran the iron pipe which carried water from the washbasin in the corner. He carefully tied one end of his improvised rope around this pipe and threw the other out into the night.

He went out feetfirst, took a firm grip on the sheets and began to slide down. The icy wind cut through the thin material of his bathrobe and the rain blinded him and then his feet bumped against the sill of the room below and he was safe.

He swayed there for a moment, hanging on to his lifeline with one trembling hand, reaching out with the other in an attempt to open the window. It was locked. He lifted his elbow recklessly and pushed it hard against the glass. A sudden gust of wind whirled round the corner, half-drowning the sound, and he reached in through the jagged hole and unfastened the catch. A moment later, he was crouched in the warm darkness.

He appeared to be in some kind of storeroom,

for the walls were lined with wooden shelves piled high with blankets. A thin strip of light drifted in at the bottom of the door and he opened it cautiously and stepped out into the deserted corridor.

He closed the door behind him and walked slowly along, his senses alert for danger. What his next move was to be, he did not know. He preferred to leave it to chance. He felt calm and fatalistic now because, in some queer way, he knew he was going to get away with it.

As he came to the end of the corridor, he heard voices talking quietly, and when he peered round the corner he saw two soldiers leaning against the wall at the stairhead. They were both armed with machine pistols.

Colonel Li was obviously taking no chances. Chavasse retraced his steps and paused suddenly as he heard voices approaching from the other end of the corridor. There was a small door at his back and he opened it quickly and stepped into darkness.

He was standing at the head of a narrow stone circular stairway that seemed to descend through the thickness of the outer wall. He went down cautiously, and when he opened the door at the bottom found himself in a long, whitewashed corridor.

He walked quickly along, checking the rooms as he did so. Suddenly he heard voices coming from behind the door at the far end. It was slightly open, and he peered in. Two soldiers were sitting at a wooden table having a meal and laughing over some joke. He continued on and turned the corner into a smaller corridor in which there were just two doors.

He opened the first one and found himself in a lavatory, but the other room was more promising. It contained five beds and several tin lockers, and was obviously living quarters for some of the guards.

All the lockers contained the same things: spare uniforms, rubber boots and various personal items. He grabbed the first uniform which looked something like his size and a pair of rubber boots and started to change quickly.

When he was ready, he examined himself in a cracked mirror. In the drab, quilted uniform he would pass anywhere, with a little luck. He needed only one extra touch.

He found what he was looking for in the end locker. It was a uniform cap with the Red Star of the army of the People's Republic set above the peak and he pulled it forward over his eyes to obscure as much of his face as possible. At that moment, the door opened and a soldier walked in.

He was a young and brawny peasant with slightly bowed legs and the hands of a farmer. His jaw went slack with astonishment, and then he moved in.

Chavasse was in no condition to fight fairly.

There was an old broken chair leaning against the wall behind him. He snatched it up and smashed it down across the head and shoulders of the unfortunate intruder.

The soldier sank to his knees with a terrible groan. He tried to get up, his arms reaching out as Chavasse moved for the door. His grasping fingers clawed at the quilted uniform and Chavasse turned and kicked him in the stomach. The man went over backwards and writhed on the floor, his face slowly turning purple.

Chavasse closed the door and moved quickly along the corridor. He mounted the steps at the far end, opened another door and found himself in a narrow passage that opened into the main hall.

There was a tiny glass office by the entrance and two guards were sitting in it drinking tea. He walked steadily forward, keeping his head down, and one of the guards looked over his shoulder, called something and laughed, exposing decaying yellow teeth. Chavasse waved a hand casually and went out into the night.

A jeep was parked at the bottom of the steps, its canvas hood raised against the rain. He hesitated for only a moment before going down the steps quickly and climbing behind the wheel. The engine roared into life at the first touch of the accelerator and he released the handbrake and drove slowly away.

He waited for the sound to come from behind,

for the sudden cries of alarm, but nothing happened. There was a soldier on duty under the light at the main entrance, a submachine gun crooked in his arm. Chavasse slowed to stop, but the man raised an arm and waved him on. He turned into the square outside and drove down into the centre of Changu.

When he parked the jeep in the courtyard outside Hoffner's house, the rain was still drifting slowly down and it was cold and raw. It had been easy—almost too easy—and as he mounted the steps to the front door he felt no particular jubilation. He was tired, very tired, and curiously light-headed.

When he pulled on the chain, the bell echoed into the darkness inside. He leaned against the door and when it opened suddenly he staggered forward.

And then he was safe—truly safe. Arms reached out to steady him, soft arms, but with strength in them for all that, and Katya Stranoff's face glowed out of the half-darkness.

15

It was pleasant and far removed from the world outside, from the rain drumming against the shutters; Chavasse relaxed, the warm fire on his bare chest, and watched Katya make tea by the hearth.

Hoffner sounded him with a stethoscope, his face intent. After a while he straightened and shook his head. "You should be in hospital, Paul. Physically, you're in a terrible state."

"My condition's hardly likely to improve if I stay round here for much longer," Chavasse said. "What I need is something to keep me going for a while. Can you do anything?"

Hoffner nodded. "But only for a limited time." He turned to his black bag and took out a small glass ampoule and a syringe.

"How long will that last?" Chavasse asked.

"Under ordinary circumstances, twenty-four hours," Hoffner said, "but in the state you're in, I can't be sure. I can give you this and one more. Two days at the most. After that you'll be flat on your back."

"But safe across the border into Kashmir."

He hardly felt the needle go in, and as soon as it was withdrawn he started to dress again hurriedly. Katya turned and handed him scalding tea in a porcelain bowl and he raised it to his mouth and drank greedily.

"When do you intend to leave?" she said.

He frowned. "When do *I* intend to leave? But we're *all* going."

She placed a hand on his knee and said earnestly, "*You* must try to get out, Paul, that I can understand, but Doctor Hoffner is an old man. It's at least a hundred and forty miles from here to the border, over rough country. He'll never make it."

"I've got a military jeep standing in the courtyard with a tankful of petrol," Chavasse said. "We can drive from here to the other side of Rudok, leaving the jeep at the foot of the Pangong Tso Pass and go through on foot for the last two or three miles."

"But his heart won't be able to stand the altitude," she insisted.

Hoffner brought her to her feet and placed his hands on her shoulders. "Katya, I've got to go.

You must understand that, but I want you to come with us more than anything else in the world."

Chavasse buttoned his quilted tunic and stood up. "I'd like to remind you that we haven't got much time. They'll discover I'm missing within the next half hour at the outside."

She shook her head. "But why is it so imperative? There's something here I don't understand."

Hoffner glanced at Chavasse, eyebrows raised, and Chavasse nodded. The old man looked down at her and said gently, "I'm afraid we haven't been completely honest with you, my dear. You see, I've made a discovery of some importance. A significant new contribution to mathematical concept."

"And that's the understatement of the age," Chavasse said.

Hoffner ignored him and continued, "This discovery means that I have suddenly become important, not only to my own country, but to the entire Western world."

Her face was completely expressionless, and yet there was pain in her eyes. "Why didn't you tell me this before? Didn't you trust me? Do I mean so little to you?" She turned to Chavasse. "To either of you?"

"But it would be asking so much," Hoffner said. "To turn against your own people. To live amongst strangers for the rest of your life."

She lifted one of his hands and held it against her cheek. "You are my people." She turned and smiled straight at Chavasse. "You and Paul. Who else have I got in all the world?"

Chavasse pulled her into his arms and when he kissed her, her face was wet with tears. She smiled happily as she looked up at him, and then her smile died.

He felt a cold breath of wind from the outer hall as it touched the nape of his neck, and something seemed to crawl up his spine. He pushed Katya away and turned slowly. Captain Tsen stood just inside the doorway, Hoffner's Chinese houseboy beside him, a machine pistol in his hand.

There was an expression of unholy joy on Tsen's face and his teeth gleamed in the firelight. "So, at last we have the truth, Mr. Chavasse? I'm sure you'll agree it was well worth our little stratagem, but now the playacting is over."

He should have known, Chavasse told himself bitterly. The whole damn thing had been too easy. To Colonel Li, who knew his man, the escape was something he had counted on. Just another move in the game, and one that had paid off.

Hoffner took a step forward, pushing Chavasse to one side. "Now look here, Captain," he began.

"Please stay exactly where you are," Tsen told him coldly.

For a brief moment the houseboy's eyes flickered towards Hoffner, and it was all Chavasse needed. He gave Katya a push that sent her staggering out of harm's way and dived for the safety of the shadows behind a wing-backed chair.

As the houseboy swung the machine pistol in an arc, bullets spraying the furniture, Katya ran forward shouting, "No, Paul, no!" and then she screamed and fell to the floor.

She lay on the sheepskin rug in front of the fire, blood pouring over her face from a wound in her forehead. Chavasse crouched for a moment to the side of the chair and peered round the edge.

211

The houseboy and Tsen were still standing in the doorway and Hoffner was kneeling over Katya. "You can't get away, Chavasse," Tsen cried. "Come out with your hands up."

Chavasse crawled on his belly behind an antique divan and carefully lifted a small Chinese ornament from a table beside him. He hefted it in his hand for a moment.

"I'm running out of patience," Tsen cried.

Chavasse lobbed the ornament across the room into the shadows of the far corner. The houseboy turned and fired twice in rapid succession and Chavasse stood up, took three quick paces forward and hit him across the back of the neck with the edge of his hand. He grabbed the machine pistol as it fell from nerveless fingers.

Tsen had only just managed to get his automatic out. He dropped it hurriedly and Chavasse bent to pick it up and slipped it into his pocket.

"There's only one thing keeping you alive," he said. "The fact that I happen to have a use for you. Now take off your belt and turn round."

Tsen complied, hate and fear in his eyes, and Chavasse tied his wrists together behind his back with the strap and pushed him down in a chair.

He went and stood over Hoffner and Katya. The old man had his black medical bag on the floor and was gently swabbing blood away from her face.

"How bad is it?" Chavasse asked.

"She's a lucky girl," Hoffner told him. "The bullet has simply grazed her. She'll be unconscious for some time and when she wakes up, she'll be suffering from shock and possibly confusion."

"Can she travel? That's the important thing."

Hoffner shrugged and started to unroll a bandage. "She'll have to—we can't leave her here after this."

Chavasse laid the machine pistol on the floor beside him. "I'll get the necessary clothing and so on from the bedrooms. I'll leave you the gun in case our friend tries to give you any trouble."

When he returned five minutes later with several sheepskin coats and quilted jackets in his arms, Hoffner had just finished bandaging Katya's head and was in the act of giving her an injection.

He closed his bag quickly and stood up. "Well, she's as ready as she'll ever be."

Chavasse lifted her gently from the ground and Hoffner slipped her arms into the sleeves of a quilted jacket and then a heavy sheepskin coat, pulling the hood up around her head.

Chavasse carried her out to the jeep while Hoffner got himself ready. It was still raining outside, and a cold wind was blowing. Chavasse made Katya as comfortable as he could on the rear bench seat and then hurried back inside.

Hoffner stood in the centre of the room dressed in a long sheepskin coat and fur cap with earflaps, the machine pistol in his right hand looking somehow incongruous and out of place.

There was a slight frown on his face, but it suddenly cleared and he crossed to his desk, opened one of its cupboards and took out a worn leather briefcase. "I mustn't forget this, of all things."

"The papers?" The old man nodded and Chavasse asked, "Anything else?"

Hoffner looked around the room and sighed. "So very many years." He shook his head sadly. "I think I'd like to leave everything exactly as it is. I've never believed in the erection of senti-mental monuments, and I'm too old to start now." He picked up his medical bag.

Tsen still sat huddled in his seat, and he glared at them malevolently. "You'll never get away with this."

213

"Oh, but we will," Chavasse said, pulling him to his feet, "because you're going to sit beside me as we go right through the gates."

Tsen suddenly looked as if he were going to be sick, but Chavasse remembered Joro and there was no pity in his heart. He sent Tsen staggering out into the hall with a powerful shove and followed.

When they reached the jeep Hoffner got into the rear seat beside Katya and Chavasse took the wheel, Tsen sitting beside him.

The streets were completely deserted as they rolled through the town. As they approached the gate, Chavasse brought the automatic out of his pocket and held it in his lap.

"Remember to say the right things," he said warningly.

There was no sentry box and the soldier who stood under the lantern by the closed gates looked the picture of misery as the rain beat down on him.

Chavasse slowed and the soldier moved forward, burp gun shining in the headlights. Tsen leaned out and cried, "Get the gates open, you dolt, I'm in a hurry."

The man's jaw dropped in dismay and he turned at once and lifted the great swing bar which secured the gates. He pulled them back quickly and stood to one side.

Chavasse kept his head down as they went by, the peak of the military cap shading his face. He turned once to look back and saw the gates beginning to close and then he moved into top gear and drove forward into the night.

Dogs barked as they passed through the camp of the herdsmen and then they were climbing up out of the valley, leaving Changu in the darkness below.

About twenty minutes later, Chavasse braked to a halt and turned to Tsen. "Get out."

"But my wrists," Tsen pleaded. "How can I walk all the way back?"

"I said get out!" Chavasse told him coldly.

As Tsen scrambled to the ground and started back along the track, Chavasse got out and went after him.

"Captain Tsen!" he called. "I was forgetting something. A debt I owe you, for myself and a lot of other people."

As Tsen turned warily, Chavasse pulled the automatic from his pocket and shot him twice through the head at close quarters.

For a moment he stood over the body, then he returned to the jeep and, disregarding Hoffner's shocked face, drove away into the night.

16

In the grey of the early dawn, the walls of Yalung Gompa were a vivid splash of orange against the storm-filled skies. Chavasse frowned in puzzlement. There was something different about the place, something not quite right. As they drove down into the valley, he realized what it was: There was no encampment under the walls.

The whole place had a strange, neglected air about it. It was as if they were approaching some ancient ruined city, empty and forlorn. He drove slowly through the great open gates into the courtyard and braked to a halt at once.

A line of saffron-clad monks sprawled against the far wall, some with fingers digging into the dirt, others with knees drawn up to their bellies as if they had died hard.

"Oh, my God," said Hoffner, and there was horror in his voice.

"This gives you a mild idea of how the Chinese are trying to run this country," Chavasse told him. "You stay here. I'm going to have a look round."

Earlier, in a compartment in the dashboard, he had discovered an excellent military map of the area, two stick grenades and a canvas belt of .45 ammunition, obviously intended for the machine gun which was usually mounted in the rear. He quickly reloaded the machine pistol, put a handful of rounds in his pocket and crossed the courtyard to the main door.

It was cold and dark inside and he moved along a stone-flagged passage cautiously. From somewhere near at hand he could hear a low, monotonous voice raised in prayer, and he ducked through a small door and found himself in the central temple.

Candles burned beneath a great golden Buddha and a monk knelt there in prayer. He got to his feet and turned and Chavasse looked down into the familiar parchment face of the abbot, the old man whom he had found sitting beside his bed when he had awakened from his deep sleep after Kurbsky's death a thousand years ago.

"I am happy to see you," the abbot said calmly.

"And I you. What happened here?"

"The Chinese have decreed that all monasteries must close. We knew our turn would come sooner or later. They came yesterday. A strong force of cavalry."

"But what about Joro's men?" Chavasse demanded. "Couldn't they help you?"

The old man shook his head. "They left two weeks ago to join forces with a stronger group in the south."

His wise eyes stared up at Chavasse and he placed a hand on his shoulder. "But you, my son. You are a changed man. You have passed through the furnace."

"Joro is dead," Chavasse said.

The abbot nodded. "The time comes for all men. There is no escape. Can I do anything to help you?"

Chavasse shook his head. "Not now. I'm trying to cross the border into Kashmir with two friends. I'd been hoping Joro's men would help."

"A family passed through here two days ago," the abbot said. "Kazakhs from Sinkiang. A chieftain, his wife and two children. They also were hoping to cross into Kashmir. They had horses with them, which slowed them down. Perhaps you will catch up."

Chavasse nodded. "I'll have to go now." He hesitated. "Is there anything I can do for you?"

The abbot smiled tranquilly and shook his head. "Nothing, my son."

He turned and dropped to his knees again, and his low monotonous voice filled the echoing hall as Chavasse walked away.

He climbed behind the wheel of the jeep and turned to look at Katya. "How's she doing?"

"She has passed into a deep sleep," Hoffner said. "She should come out of it during the next few hours. Did you find anyone?"

Chavasse nodded. "The old abbot. He insisted on staying, I'm afraid." He started the engine. "We'll have to get moving. Colonel Li must be hot on our scent by now."

"Will he have many men with him, do you think?"

Chavasse shook his head as he drove out through the gates. "His only chance of catching us is to use his jeeps, and he's only got two. At the most, he could have ten men with him."

"Isn't there a garrison at Rudok?" Hoffner asked.

"According to Joro, ten men and a sergeant, but this is a bad security area. They stick pretty close to home."

"But surely Colonel Li will be in touch with them by radio?"

"They may not even have one. It's astonishing how primitive the Chinese can be about some things." Chavasse shrugged. "In any case, they haven't much hope of finding us in these steppes."

"I see," Hoffner said, frowning. "Do you really think we stand a chance of getting out?"

"People are doing it all the time," Chavasse told him. "Kashmir is full of refugees. As a matter of fact, the abbot told me a Kazakh family from Sinkiang passed through Yalung Gompa two days ago heading for the border. We might come across them near the pass. They could be a real help on the way through."

"But I don't understand," Hoffner said. "Why should they want to leave Sinkiang? The Kazakhs have lived there for generations."

"Colonel Li's really been keeping you in the dark, Doctor," Chavasse said. "In 1951, the Kazakhs tried to set up their own government. The Chinese called them together to talk things over, and then butchered them."

Hoffner frowned. "What happened then?"

"They've been trying to get out ever since, in large groups and single families. There were still quite a few in Kashmir when I came through, and the Turkish government has settled a lot of them on the Anatolian Plateau."

"It would seem I've been more cut off from the mainstream of events than I had imagined," Hoffner said rather bitterly. He leaned back in his seat, a frown on his face, and made no further attempt at conversation.

About two hours later it started to snow in great powdery flakes that stuck to the wind-screen, prompting Chavasse to switch on the wipers.

They crossed the great military road to Yarkand, and a little while after that Chavasse looked out and saw on his right the lake where Kerensky had landed the Beaver that night which seemed so long ago now.

He wondered if the Pole had made it back to base, and grinned suddenly. There was a man he really wanted to have another drink with.

Suddenly, Katya moaned and stirred and Hoffner touched Chavasse on the shoulder. "She's waking, Paul."

Chavasse brought the jeep to a halt and turned quickly. The rose had left her cheeks and beneath the bandage, the face seemed all hollows.

Noting that the great sheepskin coat looked far too big for Katya, he smiled down at her. "Hello, angel."

There was puzzlement in her dark eyes and she tried to struggle up, but Hoffner pushed her down gently. "No, Katya," he said. "You need rest. All the rest you can get."

She pushed his restraining hand away, sat up and looked out at the barren landscape and the steadily falling snow. "But I don't understand. Where are we?"

"Somewhere north of Rudok, about thirty miles from the border," Chavasse told her, and grinned. "We're almost home and dry."

She frowned and put a hand to her bandage. "What happened back there?"

"There was a fight at the house and a bullet grazed you," Hoffner said soothingly. "There's nothing for you to worry about. Just relax. You'll need all your strength for the final haul."

She leaned back in the corner, pulling the hood of her sheepskin coat up around her face. Chavasse turned to reach for the starter and Hoffner tapped him urgently on the shoulder.

"Just a moment. I thought I heard something."

Chavasse waited, a slight frown on his face, and then, quite clearly from somewhere behind them, the sound of an engine was carried on the wind.

Katya leaned forward. "What is it?"

"Colonel Li, hot on our trail by the sound of it," Chavasse told her grimly, then drove quickly away.

Hoffner shouted above the roar of the engine, "He must be pushing hard."

"Of course he is," Chavasse replied. "If we get away, he's faced with failure and disgrace, and his career's ruined. It might even mean his life."

"Of all alternatives, I think the last one would hurt him least," Hoffner said.

Chavasse didn't bother to reply because, suddenly, he found it was all he could do to keep to the ancient caravan trail they were following. It dropped down through a narrow ravine and its ruts were ice-bound and iron-hard.

The ravine widened and the trail dropped steeply towards a great gorge that cut its way through the heart of the rising mountain, and far below he saw a bridge.

He paused for a moment to examine the map and then engaged low gear and began a cautious descent. The cantilever bridge was a spindly, narrow affair supported by wooden beams on each side of the gorge.

He braked to a halt, jumped down to the frozen ground, walked out onto the bridge and stood in the centre for a moment. The river that splashed idly over great boulders was only about twenty feet below, but it was far enough. He turned and ran back to the jeep.

"Will it hold?" Hoffner asked.

"Solid as a rock," Chavasse said, trying to make it sound convincing. "It would take a three-ton truck easily."

There was only a couple of feet of clearance on either side as he drove slowly forward. He could feel the sweat soaking his shirt as the planks creaked ominously in the centre and then they were through and safe on the other side.

There was still one thing to be done and he braked to a halt, grabbed one of the stick grenades and walked back to the bridge. He pulled the pin and tossed the grenade out into the centre and turned his back as the explosion shattered the peace.

Pieces of stone and wooden girder lifted skywards and when he looked back, he saw that the entire middle section of the bridge had fallen in. He moved forward, waiting for the smoke to clear to get a better look. At that moment, two jeeps moved out of the mouth of the ravine on the opposite side of the river and started down the slope.

The first one carried perhaps half a dozen men and a light machine gun was mounted in the rear. He was aware of these things and his brain took account of them even as he turned and ran back to the jeep.

The wheels skidded on the icy mud and for a moment panic seized him, and then they were moving up out of the gorge. He recklessly changed to a higher gear and pressed his foot flat on the board so that the jeep bounded over the rim of the gorge, all four wheels leaving the ground as the machine gun chattered, kicking up dirt and stones to one side of them.

Once over the top, the track circled the base of a great pillar of rock. Chavasse accelerated and swung the wheel to take them round the shoulder and then Katya screamed a warning and he slammed his foot hard on the brake.

But he was too late. The track was washed out in a great sliding scoop that ran over the edge into space. The front wheels dipped into the hole and the jeep slewed towards the edge. He frantically tugged at the handbrake. For an instant, it seemed as if it might hold, and then the jeep lurched and one of the front wheels dipped over the edge.

They had only seconds in which to act. He jumped to the ground, turned and helped Katya down, then Hoffner after her, his black bag clutched firmly against his chest.

At that moment there was a protesting, shuddering groan and the jeep started to slide. Chavasse reached in, grabbed the machine pistol and the stick grenade and jumped back as the vehicle slid over the edge.

It hung there for a moment and then disappeared. There were three terrible, metal-wrenching crashes as it bounced its way down into the valley, and then silence.

Chavasse moved back along the track and peered round the edge of the bluff. The wind was beginning to sweep snow across the steppes in a great curtain, but he could see quite clearly the two jeeps parked on the other side of the bridge and the soldiers moving down on foot to cross the river.

He returned to the others. "It doesn't look too good. They're crossing the gorge on foot."

Katya looked strained and anxious, but Hoffner seemed extraordinarily composed. "What do we do now, Paul?"

"According to the map, we're only about ten miles from the border," Chavasse told him. "If we leave the track here and cross over the shoulder of the mountain, we'll come into the Pangong Tso Pass. About two miles along it, there's an old Tibetan customs post marked. There may be soldiers there, of course, but we'll have to risk that."

"It's impossible, Paul," Katya cried, the wind whipping her voice into a scream. "I couldn't walk a mile in this state. Neither could the doctor."

He grabbed her arm and urged her up the slope. "We don't have any choice."

Hoffner took her other arm and they moved upwards, heads bowed against the driving snow. They paused for a moment in the shelter of some rocks and Hoffner turned suddenly, his face grey.

"My briefcase, Paul. I left it in the jeep."

Chavasse stared blankly at him and then rage gripped him by the throat, threatening to choke him. Everything he had worked for, all the suffering of the past weeks—all for nothing.

Hoffner grabbed his arm. "It doesn't matter, Paul. It's all here in my head, that's the important thing."

"That won't matter a damn if Colonel Li gets his hands on those papers," Chavasse said. "Don't you realize that?" He pushed the stick grenade into the old man's hand. "Here, I know you aren't much with a gun. If anyone comes at you, just pull out the pin and throw it at them."

He turned, the machine pistol in his left hand, and slid back down the slope to the track. The slope continued on the other side and he went over without hesitation, glissading down to the wrecked jeep forty feet below, squeezed between great boulders.

He found the briefcase almost at once, wedged

227

under the crumpled driving seat, and he pulled it out and started back up the slope. His heart was pounding and there was blood in his mouth, but he held the briefcase and machine pistol in his left hand and pulled himself up with his right.

He scrambled over the edge of the track and started across. He slipped and fell to one knee and as he got up, he heard voices shouting through the falling snow.

He turned and looked down the track quickly as half a dozen soldiers came round the corner of the bluff, bunched together. He dropped to one knee, braced the machine pistol across his arm and loosed the whole magazine in one continuous burst. He continued across the track and scrambled up the slope, his heart heaving like some hunted animal's.

He heard the shouts of the men behind him as they started to follow and then the stick grenade he had given Hoffner sailed over his head down to the soldiers and there was an explosion. As it died away, he heard not the sounds of pursuit, but the cries of the wounded and dying.

He had no strength left. For a moment he lay there on his face, and suddenly the snow balled up around him, hiding the valley below.

He scrambled wearily to his feet as hooves clattered over loose stones and a horse moved down the slope to meet him.

The man who sat on its back wore a fur hat,

the robe of a snow leopard and soft black boots. A rifle was crooked in one arm.

Chavasse stared helplessly up at him and then the brown, handsome face split into a wide grin.

17

The snow was a living thing whipped by high wind across the steppes, but down in the hollow between the tall rocks it was strangely quiet.

Chavasse sat with his back to one of the boulders and bared his arm so that Hoffner could give him another injection. Osman Sherif, the Kazakh chieftain, squatted beside him, rifle across his knees, and grinned.

"The ways of Allah are strange, my friend," he said in Chinese. "It would seem we are fated to make the last stage of our journey together."

Behind him beside the horses stood his wife, together with Katya. The chieftain's two young children, heavily muffled in furs, were already mounted, one behind the other.

Chavasse rolled down his sleeve and stood up

"If we don't get moving soon, we might not even reach the border."

Osman Sherif looked up through the falling snow at the sky and shook his head. "I think things will get worse before they get better. I had intended making camp here for the night. It is a good place."

"Not with Chinese troops liable to arrive at any moment," Chavasse told him.

"But we cannot cross the border before nightfall," the Kazakh said.

"We don't need to," Chavasse said. "If we carry on over the shoulder of the mountain, we come into the Pangong Tso Pass. About two miles from the border, there's an old Tibetan customs post. It can't be more than six or seven miles from here. We could rest and cross over later."

"What if there are Chinese there?"

"That's a chance we have to take. In any case, there wouldn't be more than half a dozen of them." He turned to Hoffner. "What do you think, Doctor?"

"I don't see that we have any other choice," Hoffner said.

Osman Sherif shrugged. "It is with Allah. It will mean that we must leave many of our personal possessions behind so that each of you may have a horse."

"Don't worry about that," Chavasse said. "When we reach Kashmir, you'll be well taken care of. I'll see to it personally that you're transported to Turkey to join the rest of your countrymen on the Anatolian Plateau."

Sudden warmth glowed deep in the Kazakh's eyes. "You should have mentioned that earlier, my friend." He slung his rifle over one shoulder and started to unbuckle the load on the first packhorse.

Chavasse moved across to Katya and smiled down at her. "How do you feel?"

She looked alarmingly pale and her eyes had sunk deep into dark sockets. "I'll be all right, Paul. Don't worry about me. Are we going to make it?"

He patted her reassuringly on the shoulder. "We'll make it all right, don't worry about that," and then he went and helped the Kazakh with the horses.

When they rode out of the hollow ten minutes later, Osman Sherif was leading the small column and Chavasse bringing up the rear.

The horses sank to their fetlocks in the deep snow and Chavasse rode with his head bowed against the wind, alone with his thoughts. He wasn't afraid any longer. He was calmly certain that he would survive anything that was to come, even the menace of the man who followed him somewhere back there in the wind and snow.

He started to think about Colonel Li, remembering the endless interrogations and the strange, perverted friendship the other had tried to create between them. The habit he had seized on from the very beginning, for instance, of calling him Paul, as if they were good friends. As if they might conceivably have something in common.

Any possibility of friendship was doomed from the start, of course. It was just another of Li's psychological tricks that hadn't worked. And yet the man had seemed almost sincere. That was the most incredible thing about the whole affair.

A sharp stab of pain cut into his face and he winced and reined in his mount. To his surprise he found that the horse was almost knee-deep in snow, and when he wrenched off his glove and touched his face he felt caked snow and ice on his cheeks and discovered that the flesh had split in several places.

He frowned and pulled on his gloves and then panic ran through him quickly because when he raised his eyes, he saw that he was alone and that darkness was falling.

He had paused beside a great black finger of rock standing on its own like some silent sentinel, and already the wind was whipping the snow into a frenzy, obscuring the tracks left by the others. As he urged his horse forward, they disappeared completely.

For what seemed like hours he rode blindly on, trusting to the instinct of the horse, and the wind spun around his head and sliced at his cheeks until his face was so numb, he could feel no more pain.

He raised his head as his horse came to a halt. Rearing out of the gloom, thrusting upwards into the falling snow was the black finger of rock he had passed at least an hour earlier. He had been travelling in a circle.

He lowered his head against a sudden blast of wind and when he looked down at the ground, he saw great slurred prints in the snow. He urged his weary mount forward so that he could follow them.

The wind was howling like a banshee and he was completely covered with frozen snow, but he kept his head bowed and his eyes on the ground and after a while he saw a fur glove.

235

The cold had chilled his brain and his mind worked at half its normal speed. He examined his hands. He was wearing gloves; therefore, to whom did this glove belong?

A little farther on, he came across a Chinese military fur cap. He dismounted and picked it up and stared at it uncomprehendingly, and then a figure emerged from the whirling darkness and staggered into him.

Chavasse dimly discerned a frozen white mask and when he looked down at the hand that rested on his shoulder, he saw that it was bare and frozen.

He raised his glove and wiped snow from the face before him and gazed into the vacant, expressionless eyes of Colonel Li. Chavasse stood there for a long moment looking at him and then he pulled off his glove and reached into the right-hand pocket of his sheepskin coat for the automatic he had taken from Captain Tsen.

He brought it out, his finger already tightening over the trigger, and held it against Li's chest. Quite suddenly, he put it back in his pocket and pulled on his glove.

Why don't I kill you, you bastard? Why don't I kill you? There was no answer—nothing that would have made any sense—and he dragged Colonel Li unresistingly towards the horse and tried to lift him up into the saddle.

But it was no good. He didn't have that kind of strength anymore. He leaned against the horse, one arm around his enemy's shoulders, and there was a coldness on his face, a sense of limitless distance, and he felt his remaining strength ebbing.

But something white-hot still burned deep inside him, some essence of courage that refused to allow him to give in. He took a deep breath and made a final and supreme effort, which ended in Li hanging head-foremost across the horse. As Chavasse pulled himself up into the high wooden saddle and urged the beast forward, Osman Sherif came riding out of the storm to meet him.

18

The hut was low-roofed and built of great blocks of rough stone. Outside, the wind howled through the pass all the way from Mongolia, piling snow against the walls in great drifts.

It was more like a stable than anything else, with the horses occupying at least half of the available space, and Chavasse sat in a daze drinking hot tea from a bowl while steam rose from his sheepskin coat.

On the other side of the fire Katya, utterly exhausted, slept beside the two children, and their mother waited patiently for more water to boil in an iron pot.

In the corner farthest from the door, a small butter lamp flickered in a niche, and in its feeble light, Hoffner and Osman Sherif crouched over

Colonel Li. He groaned several times and Hoffner spoke soothingly to him; once he reared up convulsively and the Kazakh had to force him down again.

After a while the old man got to his feet and returned to the fire, instructing Osman Sherif to cover the Chinese with a sheepskin.

"How is he?" Chavasse said.

Hoffner sighed. "I've had to amputate three fingers on his left hand. A drastic step, but better than gangrene. It's a good thing Osman Sherif found you when he did."

The wind roared through the great tunnel of the pass and Chavasse shuddered. "We wouldn't have lasted long outside on a night like this. He's quite a man. It took a lot of guts to come looking for me in that blizzard. I'd already circled back on my own tracks when I found Colonel Li."

Hoffner filled his pipe slowly and frowned. "I used to think I understood him rather well, but now I'm not so sure. I wonder what drove him on to follow us on foot in such appalling weather."

"God knows. The workings of the Communist mind are too complicated for my understanding."

Osman Sherif squatted beside them and grinned as his wife handed him a bowl of tea. "You make things too complicated; that is the trouble with you Westerners. Out here, our values are more basic. The hunter never stops following his quarry until he has made the kill or is himself dead."

Hoffner shook his head and said softly, "No, there's more to it than that in this case. It needed something stronger to drive a man on in the state Colonel Li was in."

"It's perfectly simple," Chavasse told him. "He was after the briefcase."

"But how could he have been? Captain Tsen didn't get a chance to report back to him." Hoffner shook his head and said gently, "I think it was you he wanted, Paul."

"He was after all of us," Chavasse said. "That's obvious."

Hoffner shook his head again. "I meant something more than that, but it doesn't matter now." He leaned back, his head on his briefcase, and pulled a sheepskin coat over his body. "I think I'll get a little sleep."

Chavasse stretched out beside him and stared into the fire and tried to make some sense out of it all, but there was no answer. Or none that he could think of. After a while, he drifted into sleep.

He awakened and lay for several moments staring up at the low roof, trying to decide where he was. So many places, he thought. So very many places, and where am I now? As realization came, he tried to sit up.

His hands were swollen and chapped and his

face hurt. He touched his cheeks and winced as his fingers probed great splits in the flesh.

Everyone seemed to be asleep and he leaned forward to stir the embers into life. As the flames leapt up he saw that Katya was crouching beside Colonel Li.

She looked pale and ill as she picked her way between the sleeping bodies and sat down beside him, holding her hands out to the blaze.

"How are you feeling?" she said.

"I'll survive. How's our friend?"

"I couldn't sleep and heard him groaning. I thought I'd better take a look. What's wrong with his hand?"

"Frostbite," Chavasse said. "Doctor Hoffner had to amputate three fingers."

Her breath hissed sharply between her teeth and he put an arm around her shoulders. "I know this has all seemed like some terrible nightmare, but it won't last much longer. As soon as the weather clears, we can move across the border."

For a little while there was silence and then she said, "Paul, why do you think he continued to follow us alone and on foot in such awful weather?"

"Whatever it was, it must have been eating him up inside," Chavasse said. "Hoffner thinks it was me he was really after, not the rest of you."

She turned, a slight frown on her face. "What did he mean by that?"

He shrugged. "In Colonel Li you have a man

who lies by faith as much as any priest, but faith in the political creed on which he has based his life."

"But what has all this to do with you?"

"I can only guess. I think that for some strange personal reason, it was of supreme importance to him that I not only confess my crimes against the People's Republic, but that I also become a sincere convert to Communism through his agency."

"What makes you think that?"

"Because I believe he likes me, God help him." Chavasse sighed. "I think that in another time and place we could have been friends."

There was a long silence before Katya said softly, "And what happens now?"

Chavasse shook his head. "I don't really know. I've shaken his faith in his belief, because I refused to accept it, even under coercion. He can't continue in that state of mind. Now he has no choice. If he fails to destroy me, he destroys himself."

"Strange," she said with a frown. "You speak of him with words that suggest compassion, and yet there is no kindness in your voice."

"Pity's the last thing I feel for him. There's too much blood on his hands for that."

"What will you do with him when you leave?"

"Give him one of the horses and a little food. He can make it from here to Rudok easily if he wants to. I'm not going to kill him if that's what you mean. There's no longer any need."

241

"Because you will have destroyed him anyway?"

He nodded. "Something like that."

She gazed into the fire in silence for a while. "And what about me, Paul? What will happen when we cross over into Kashmir?"

He smiled and gently kissed her on the cheek. "I'm sure we'll find a use for you."

"You think there is hope for us, then?" Her face was like a young girl's, the eyes probing into his very soul.

"There's always hope, Katya," he said. "That's what makes life worthwhile."

She laid her head on his chest and he held her close. After a while, she drifted into sleep and he sat there staring into the flames and waiting for the dawn.

Just before morning the wind died and Osman Sherif went outside. When he came back, he was smiling. "The snow has stopped. We should be able to cross over without any difficulty."

As he started to lead the horses out through the door everyone stirred and, in a few moments, his wife had blown the fire into life and was heating water for tea.

Chavasse went out to help saddle the horses and told him that he wanted to leave one of the animals behind for Colonel Li.

"It would be wasting a good horse," the Kazakh said.

Chavasse frowned. "Don't you think he can make it to Rudok on his own?"

The Kazakh shook his head. "I mean something different. I have looked into his eyes, my friend. He is a dead man walking."

Chavasse went back inside the hut and sat down beside Hoffner, who was drinking tea. The old man looked grey and haggard, but he seemed in remarkably good spirits.

"You look pretty grim, Paul," he said cheerfully.

"You don't look so marvellous yourself," Chavasse told him, and held out his hand for the bowl of tea Osman Sherif's wife passed to him.

Katya sat beside the children on the other side of the fire, staring vacantly into the flames. She looked ill and her skin was stretched tightly over the prominent cheekbones.

"Not long now," Chavasse told her softly.

She came out of her reverie with a start. For a moment, she stared at him as if he were a stranger, a puzzled frown on her face, and then she smiled. A strange, sad smile that touched something deep inside him.

He emptied his bowl, filled it again and went and squatted beside Colonel Li, who sat with his back against a wall, a sheepskin across his legs.

Li held his bandaged hand against his chest and seemed quite calm in spite of his pallor. He smiled tightly as he accepted the tea. "I suppose I should congratulate you."

"One thing still puzzles me," Chavasse said. "Why didn't Tsen have troops to back him up when he was waiting for me to turn up at Hoffner's house?"

Colonel Li smiled faintly. "Six men were detailed to report to him at midnight, but I'm afraid the speed with which you escaped wrecked our plans. Did any of my men survive? There were three with me when I set out."

"We didn't see any. I was lost in the blizzard myself when I ran into you." Osman Sherif came in and squatted beside the fire, and Chavasse nodded towards him. "You owe your life to our friend there."

Colonel Li emptied the bowl and placed it carefully on the ground beside him. "But not for long, I imagine."

Chavasse shook his head. "You've got it all wrong. We're leaving you a horse and some food. You should be able to reach Rudok easily."

Colonel Li's lips twitched slightly and suddenly there was sweat on his forehead. "You mean you're not going to shoot me?"

Chavasse shook his head. "There's no need, Colonel. As our American friends would say, you're all washed up."

He started to get to his feet and a quiet voice said, "Not quite, Paul."

He turned very slowly. Katya was standing on the other side of the fire facing all of them. In her hands, she held the machine pistol.

Hoffner was the first to speak. "Katya, for God's sake! What does this mean?"

Her extreme pallor only made her more beautiful. The skin of her face was almost translucent and the dark sad eyes held a haunted expression Chavasse was to remember for the rest of his days.

He moved forward slightly, hands thrust deep into the pockets of his sheepskin coat, and smiled softly. "Tell him, angel. Tell him everything."

Suddenly there was something that was almost horror in her eyes. "You knew," she whispered. "You knew all the time. But if that's true, why did you bring me with you?"

"My people would have found you a prize package. They don't use the same methods as your side to extract information, but they're even more successful. I've been waiting for you to show your hand ever since you recovered consciousness," Chavasse said. "It was your boyfriend here who let you down, if you're interested. When he exposed my little masquerade at Hoffner's house that afternoon, he said that he and Kurbsky had run into each other at a village called Rangong a few days earlier. Unfortunately, Kurbsky had already told me they'd never met."

"We all make mistakes," she said.

"Not in this game—not if you want to stay alive, anyway," he told her. "And the pair of you made two. When we were out riding, I told you I'd helped the Dalai Lama out of Tibet. I knew for a fact that Peking couldn't have known I was involved and yet Colonel Li did. You were the only person who could have been his source of information. You certainly mix with the right people."

"It wasn't difficult—he is my brother," she said proudly. "We know what we are doing and where we are going."

"For God's sake, don't give me any more of that claptrap," Chavasse said. "I've had my bellyful during the past few weeks. Would it be too much to ask why you were planted on the doctor?"

"He was important to us as a figurehead, because the people trusted him." She shrugged. "It was necessary for some reliable person to share his confidences. This affair alone has proved the value of my presence in the house."

"There's one small point that has been bothering me for a long time," he said. "When I tried to take a shot at your brother, my Walther jammed. I've never known them to do that before."

"I'd taken the precaution of emptying the clip the previous night," she said. "When you were asleep."

"Most efficient of you." He sighed. "You realize what will happen to us when you take us back? You know how we'll be treated?"

"They will only do what is necessary for the good of the State," she said. "Nothing more."

"Katya!" There was pain in Hoffner's voice. "Did I mean nothing more to you than that?"

"Nothing, Doctor," she said flatly.

"I don't believe you."

He started round the fire towards her and she raised the machine pistol warningly. "Keep back, Doctor. I will shoot, I promise you."

"And kill the brain," Chavasse said mockingly.

"It is all in the briefcase," she told him calmly. "I have nothing to lose."

Hoffner kept on moving, a hand stretched out towards her. "Katya, please listen to me."

"I warn you," she said.

Chavasse had been watching her index finger curl around the trigger of the machine pistol, his own hand ready on Tsen's automatic. As her knuckle whitened, he fired twice through the pocket of his sheepskin coat.

The force of the bullets lifted her back against the wall, and she dropped the machine pistol and slid down to the ground.

Hoffner gave an agonized cry, his hands going to his face, and Chavasse pushed him out of the way and knelt beside her. She stared up at him, that characteristic slight frown on her face, and then she choked as blood poured from her mouth. As he eased her down to the floor, the head lolled to one side.

Osman Sherif was already hustling his wife and their two children outside as Chavasse got to his feet and faced Hoffner.

"I'm sorry," he said. "I know how much she meant to you."

Hoffner shook his head slowly. "There was nothing else you could do. For the first time in my life I'm beginning to realize the strength of the opposition. I think we ought to do something about it."

He picked up his briefcase and doctor's bag and followed the others as Chavasse turned and looked down at Katya for the last time.

Colonel Li knelt beside her. After a moment, he got to his feet, and when he spoke, his voice seemed to belong to someone else.

"You are a hard man," he said. "Harder than I ever imagined a man could be."

"I'm a professional," Chavasse told him. "That's something you wouldn't understand, but she would. She was one herself."

He started to turn away and Li caught his arm. "Kill me, Paul!"

Chavasse jerked himself free without speaking and went outside. The sky was grey but already beginning to clear, and the snow was startlingly white.

The others were already mounted and Osman Sherif held a horse ready for him. Chavasse reached for the pommel of the high wooden saddle and pulled himself up. It was an effort, but he made it and they started to move forward.

He was aware that Colonel Li had stumbled out of the doorway to stand beside the tethered horse they had left him, but he didn't bother to look back.

The effects of Hoffner's injections were beginning to wear off and all of a sudden, he felt really tired. But it didn't matter. Nothing mattered except that in some strange way, life was now beginning all over again.

It must have been an hour later when they reached the crest of the pass. From somewhere a thousand miles away he seemed to hear his name and he turned and looked for the last time at the small figure, black against the snow beside the customs hut. He urged his horse forward and rode after the others, down into Kashmir.

LONDON
1995

19

The fire was low now, the room quiet for several moments as Chavasse finished talking. It was Moro who spoke first.

"So, you crossed into India safely, you and Dr. Hoffner and the Kazakhs?"

"That's right."

"But what happened then? No further word of Hoffner, not anywhere. I've checked all sources."

"The whole thing was handled with total secrecy, just as if he didn't exist. It was all meant to fool Chinese intelligence, of course."

"So he was taken to England?"

Chavasse nodded. "Moncrieff arranged everything. As I say, total secrecy. There was a safe house arranged in the countryside outside Cambridge where he was supposed to meet with

Professor Craig from the Joint Space Research Programme at NATO."

There was a pause. Moro said, "You said 'was supposed to.'"

"Life playing its usual bad joke. Karl Hoffner died of a heart attack on his first night in the house. He was an old man, remember; that dreadful journey and all that stress proved too much for him. Since in a manner of speaking he didn't officially exist, he had a very private cremation by the Bureau's disposal unit."

"But you had his papers, all the details of his research. Why was nothing heard of this?"

"Oh, Professor Craig and his people went to work on them. He used the best brains he could find, but they all drew a blank. Hoffner's theory was either seriously flawed or of such genius that no other mind on earth could make sense of it."

There was another silence and then Moro said, "All for nothing. That dreadful journey. Colonel Li crippled, Katya's death. So many deaths." He shook his head and said again, "All for nothing."

"That's the way it goes sometimes. Life can be pretty bloody-minded," Chavasse told him. He smiled. "A long time ago."

"Yet you are still here," Moro said. "The sole survivor, as it were."

"Not really." Chavasse reached to the coffee table, took a cigarette from a silver box and lit it. "There's always you."

This time the silence was profound. Moro's face seemed to change, almost as if he had become another person, and he slipped a hand inside his robe.

"What do you mean?"

"Let's forget your rather intimate knowledge of my background and stick with the fact that you knew about Karl Hoffner and the fact that I got him out of Tibet. Very interesting, that. When I asked you where you got your information you said from sources of your own."

"So?" Moro said.

"Let's go over it again. I crossed into India with Hoffner, and Osman Sherif and his family went to Turkey, so we can discount them. So who else knew? Professor Craig who died years ago. Sir Ian Moncrieff, also dead. No official record of the operation in the Bureau files. I know that for a fact, because I've been Chief of the Bureau for twenty years."

"I see you are a logician, Sir Paul."

"Oh, yes," Chavasse said. "I like things to make sense. So, where does this all leave us? With me being the only person in the world who knows anything about the Hoffner affair at all." He helped himself to another cigarette. "In fact, there would seem to be only one person you could have got your knowledge of Hoffner from, and according to my intelligence sources he died of cancer in Peking ten years ago." Chavasse

255

blew out smoke and leaned back in the chair, his right hand on the cushion. "Colonel Li."

Moro took a deep breath, then said, "He was my father. I was the product of a brief encounter with his Tibetan housekeeper at Changu. I was born in 1960. She died shortly after the Hoffner affair. My father took me to Peking, raised me, loved me, educated me. The university background I told you of is true; I really did go to Cambridge."

"And he told you about Hoffner. So if you knew most of it anyway, why ask me to go over it again?"

"To hear it from your own lips. Also, I have wondered all these years what kind of man you were. You killed my aunt, Katya; my father was left crippled, a claw for one hand, totally shamed. It was like acid burning into him over the years. It never went away."

"So now you want revenge? You've taken your time."

"I've dreamt of it for years. In a matter of family honour, the waiting is nothing. I knew my time would come."

Chavasse nodded. "I should tell you that when they were feeding you in the kitchen I put in a call to the temple at Glen Aristoun. They'd never heard of a Lama Moro. I also spoke to Jackson on the house phone. He's been right outside the door all this time. If you look you'll see it's slightly ajar." He raised his voice. "Come in, Earl."

The door swung open and Jackson stepped in. He closed it behind him. "I heard everything. Better than the midnight movie on TV."

Moro's hand came out of his robe clutching a pistol. He stood and backed away so that he could cover them both.

"Interesting," Chavasse said to Earl. "Chinese copy of a Russian Tokarev."

"Type 670," Jackson nodded. "Trouble with those is that when you use them in the silenced Mode you can only get one round off, and there are two of us."

"One is enough," Moro said. "I really am a monk, Sir Paul, of the Shao Lin temple. Death means nothing to me. This is for Katya and my father."

"When you intend to kill a man do it, don't talk about it," Chavasse said.

He found the silenced Walther he had placed in the cushion at his side, his hand swept up and he shot Moro twice in the heart, knocking him back against the wall. Moro dropped the Tokarev and fell to the floor. Jackson knelt down and turned him on his back.

"Dead," he said. "Two in the pumper. Good thing you check out on the range every week. This little sod was going to kill you."

"I know." Chavasse was on the phone. After a moment he said, "The Chief here. Tell Section

Three I've had a red alert at my home. Need immediate disposal team." He put the phone down. "Twenty minutes, Earl, and let's keep Lucy out of it."

"As you like, Sir Paul," Jackson said formally.

The discreet undertaker's van appeared on time. Two aging gentlemen in formal attire came to the drawing room with a coffin and departed with Moro's body. The blood had soaked into his robe and there was no stain on the carpet.

"A few pounds of grey ash," Jackson said. "That's all he'll be in the morning. They'll probably strew him on one of the grass verges."

"You're a hard man, Earl."

"Comes of soldiering too long." Jackson shrugged. "Nothing else you could have done. It was you or him. Can I get you anything?"

"No thanks."

"I'll say goodnight then."

The door closed and Chavasse sat down to think about recent events, then picked up the phone and rang Downing Street. When it was answered he said, "Code Eagle. Give me the prime minister."

A moment later John Major came on. "Paul?"

"I just wanted to let you know, Prime Minister, that I'll be at my desk tomorrow and that I'll occupy it for as long as you need me."

"Marvellous," Major told him. "We'll speak soon."

Chavasse put down the phone and poured a Bushmills, then went and drew the curtains and opened the French window. Rain drummed down on the terrace.

After all was said and done, what else was he going to do? He raised his glass and toasted the night.

If you enjoyed *Year of the Tiger*, you won't want to miss Jack Higgins's . . .

DRINK
WITH THE
DEVIL

Here is an excerpt from this exciting thriller available in bookstores from Berkley Books . . .

Keogh found the Regent Cafe with no trouble. One window was boarded up, obviously from bomb blast, but the other was intact, offering a clear view of the interior. There were hardly any customers, just three old men at one table and a ravaged-looking middle-aged woman at another, who looked like a prostitute.

The girl sitting behind the counter was just sixteen, he knew that because he knew all about her. Her name was Kathleen Ryan and she ran the cafe on behalf of her uncle, Michael Ryan, a Protestant gunman from his earliest youth. She was a small girl with black hair and angry eyes above pronounced cheekbones—not pretty by any conventional standard. She wore a dark sweater, denim miniskirt, and boots, and sat on a stool engrossed in a book when Keogh went in.

He leaned on the counter. "Is it good?"

She looked him over calmly and that look told him of someone infinitely older than her years.

"Very good. *The Midnight Court*."

"But that's in Irish surely?" Keogh reached for the book and saw that he was right.

"And why shouldn't it be? You think a Protestant shouldn't read Irish? Why not? It's our country, too, mister, and if you're Sinn Fein or any of that old rubbish I'd prefer you went elsewhere. Catholics aren't welcome. An IRA street bomb killed my father, my mother, and my wee sister."

"Girl, dear." Keogh held up his hands defensively. "I'm a Belfast boy home from the sea, who's just come in for a cup of tea."

"You don't sound Belfast to me. English I'd say."

"And that's because my father took me to live there when I was a boy."

She frowned for a moment then shrugged. "All right." She raised her voice. "Tea for one, Mary." She said to Keogh, "No more cooking. We're closing soon."

"The tea will do just fine."

A moment later, a grey-haired woman in an apron brought tea in a mug and placed it on the counter. "Milk and sugar over there. Help yourself."

Keogh did as he was told and pushed a pound

coin across. The woman gave him some change. The girl ignored him, reached for her book and stood up. "I'll be away now, Mary. Give it another hour then you can take an early night," and she went through to the back.

Keogh took his tea to a table by the door, sat down and lit a cigarette. Five minutes later Kathleen Ryan emerged wearing a beret and an old trenchcoat. She went out without looking at him. Keogh sipped some more tea, then got up and left.

It was raining harder now as she turned on to the waterfront and she increased her pace, head down. The three youths standing in the doorway of a disused warehouse saw her coming as she passed under the light of a street lamp. They were of a type to be found in any city in the world. Vicious young animals in bomber jackets and jeans.

"That's her, Pat," the one wearing a baseball cap said. "That's her. The Ryan bitch from the cafe."

"I can tell for myself, you fool," the one called Pat said. "Now hold still and grab her on the way past."

Kathleen Ryan was totally unaware of their existence as they stayed back in the shadows. It was only the quick rush of feet that alerted her and by then it was too late, one arm around her neck half choking her.

Pat walked round in front and tilted her chin. "Well, now, what have we got here? A little Prod bitch. Ryan, isn't it?"

She kicked backward, catching the youth in the baseball cap on the shin. "Leave me be, you Taig bastard."

"Taig bastard is it," Pat said. "And us decent Catholic boys!" He slapped her face. "Up the alley with her. Time she learned her manners."

She didn't scream for it was not in her nature, but cried out in rage and bit the hand that fastened on her mouth.

"Bitch!" Baseball Cap called out and punched her in the back and then they ran her along the alley through the rain. There was a stack of packing cases clear under an old-fashioned gas street lamp. As she struggled, two of them pulled her across a packing case and Pat moved up behind and racked her skirt up.

"Time you learned," he said.

"No, time you learned!" a voice called. Pat turned and Martin Keogh walked up the alley, hands in the pockets of his reefer. "Put her down. I mean, she doesn't know where you've been, does she?"

"Stuff you, wee man," the one in the baseball cap said, releasing his hold on the girl as he swung a punch at Keogh, who caught the wrist, twisted, and ran him face-first into the wall.

"You bastard!" the third youth cried and rushed him.

Keogh's left hand came out of his pocket holding the Walther and he slashed the youth across the face, splitting the cheek from the left eye to the corner of the mouth. He raised the gun and fired, the distinctive muted cough of the silenced weapon flat in the rain.

Baseball Cap was on his knees, the other clutching his cheek, blood pouring through his fingers. Pat stood there, rage on his face.

"You bloody swine!"

"It's been said before." Keogh touched him between the eyes with the silenced end of the Walther. "Not another word or I'll kill you."

267

The youth froze. Kathleen Ryan was pulling her skirt down. Keogh said, "Back to that cafe of yours, girl. I'll see you soon."

She hesitated, staring at him, then turned and ran away along the alley.

There was only the rain now and the groans of the injured. Pat said wildly, "We did what you told us to do. Why this?"

"Oh, no," Keogh said. "I told you to frighten the girl a little and then I'd come and save her." He found a cigarette one-handed and lit it. "And what were we into? Gang rape."

"She's a dirty little Prod. Who cares?"

"I do," Keogh told him. "And I'm a Catholic. You give us a bad name."

Pat rushed him. Keogh swayed to one side, tripping him with his right foot, and dropped one knee down hard in his back. Pat lay there in the rain.

Keogh said, "You need a lesson, son."

He jammed the muzzle of the Walther against the youth's thigh and pulled the trigger. There was a muted report and Pat cried out.

Keogh stood up. "Only a flesh wound. It could have been your kneecap."

Pat was sobbing now. "Damn you!"

"Taken care of a long time ago." Keogh took an envelope from his pocket and dropped it down. "Five hundred quid, that was the price. Now get yourself to the Royal Victoria Casualty Department. Best in the world for gunshot wounds, but then they get a lot of experience."

He walked away, whistling an eerie little tune and left them there in the rain.

When he reached the cafe there were no longer any customers, but he could see Kathleen Ryan and the woman Mary standing behind the counter. The girl was on the telephone. Keogh tried the door, but it was locked. Kathleen Ryan turned as the door rattled and nodded to Mary, who came from behind the counter and unlocked it.

As Keogh entered Mary said, "She told me what you did for her. God bless you."

Keogh sat on the edge of a table and lit a cigarette. The girl was still talking. "No, I'll be fine now. I'll be at the Drum in twenty minutes. Don't fret." She put the phone down and turned, her face calm. "My uncle Michael. He worries about me."

"And why not?" Keogh said. "Desperate times."

"You don't take prisoners, do you?"

"I could never see the point."

"And you're carrying. A Walther from what I saw."

"Very knowledgeable for one so young."

"Oh, I know guns, mister, I was raised on them. What did you do after I left?"

"I sent them on their way."

"Home, was it, with a pat on the head?"

"No, the nearest casualty department. They needed a lesson. They got one. The one who seemed to be in charge will be on sticks for a while if that's a comfort to you."

She frowned, her eyes dark. "What's your game?"

"No game. I didn't like what was going on, that's all." He stood up and stubbed out his cigarette. "Still, you seem fine now so I'll be on my way."

He got the door open. She said quickly, "No, hang on." He turned and she added, "You can walk me to my uncle's pub. That's the Orange Drum on Connor's Wharf. It's about a quarter of a mile. My name is Kathleen Ryan. What's yours?"

"Martin Keogh."

"Wait for me outside."

He did as he was told and saw her go to the phone again. Probably speaking to her uncle, he thought. A few moments later she joined him, this time carrying a large umbrella.

As she put it up against the driving rain he said, "And wouldn't a taxi be safer?"

"I like the city at night," she told him. "I like the rain. I've a right to go on my own way and to hell with those Fenian bastards."

"A point of view," he replied as they started to walk.

"Here, get under this," she said, pulling him under the umbrella taking his arm. "A sailor you said?"

"Just for the past couple of years."

"A sailor from Belfast raised in London who carries a Walther?"

There was a question in her voice. "A dangerous place, this old town, as you saw tonight."

"Dangerous for you, you mean, and that's why you're carrying." She frowned. "You're not a Fenian or you wouldn't have done what you did to that lot."

"I'm not anybody's, girl dear." He paused to light a cigarette.

She said, "Give me one."

"I will not, you with your green years ahead of you. God, but you're one for the questions, Kate."

She turned to glance at him. "Why do you call me that? No one else does."

"Oh, it seems to suit."

They were walking along the waterfront now, container ships anchored at the Quay and, farther out, the red and green lights of a freighter moving out to sea.

Kathleen Ryan said, "So, the gun? Why are you carrying?"

"Jesus, it's the persistent one you are. A long time ago I was a soldier. Did three tours of duty in this very town and there's always the chance of someone with a long memory and a grudge to work off."

"What regiment?"

"1 Para."

"Don't tell me you were at Bloody Sunday in Londonderry?"

"That's right. Like I said, a long time ago."

Her hand tightened on his arm. "God, but you lads gave those Fenians a roasting that day. How many did you kill? Thirteen wasn't it?"

The lights of the pub were plain across a cobbled quay now. Keogh said, "How old are you?"

"Sixteen."

"So young and so full of hate."

"I told you. The IRA killed my father, my mother, and my wee sister. That only leaves Uncle Michael."

The sign said The Orange Drum and painted

on the brick wall beside it was the legend Our Country Too. The girl put the umbrella down, opened the door, and led the way in.

The interior was a typical Belfast pub with several booths, a few tables and chairs, and a long mahogany bar. Bottles of every kind of drink were ranged on shelves against a mirrored wall. There were only a half-dozen customers, all old men, four of them playing cards by an open fire, two others talking softly to each other. A hard-looking young man with one arm sat behind the bar reading the *Belfast Telegraph*.

He glanced up and put the paper down. "Are you okay, Kathleen? Michael told me what happened."

"I'm fine, Ivor. Thanks to Mr. Keogh here. Is Uncle Michael in the back?"

At that moment a door opened and a man walked through. Keogh knew him at once from the photos Barry had supplied at his briefing in Dublin. Michael Ryan, aged fifty-five, a Loyalist of the first water who had served in the UVF and Red Hand of Ulster, the most extreme Protestant group of all, a man who had killed for his beliefs many times. He was of medium height, hair greying slightly at the temples, eyes very blue, and there was an energy to him.

"This is Martin Keogh," the girl said.

Ryan came round the bar and held out his

hand. "You did me a good turn tonight. I shan't forget."

"Lucky I was there."

"That's as may be. I owe you a drink anyway."

"Bushmills Whiskey would be fine," Keogh told him.

"Over here." Ryan indicated a booth in the corner.

The girl took off her raincoat and beret and eased behind the table. Her uncle sat beside her and Keogh was opposite. Ivor brought a bottle of Bushmills and two glasses.

"Can I get you anything, Kathleen?"

"No, I'm okay, Ivor."

He plainly worshipped her, but nodded and walked away. Ryan said, "I've checked with a contact at the Royal Victoria. They just received three very damaged young men. One with a bullet in the thigh."

"Is that a fact?" Keogh said.

Kathleen Ryan stared at him. "You didn't tell me."

"No need."

"Let's see what you're carrying," Ryan said.

"No need to worry. All friends here."

Keogh shrugged, took the Walther from his pocket and passed it across. Ryan examined it expertly. "Carswell silencer, the new job. Very nice." He took a Browning from his pocket and passed it over. "Still my personal favourite."

"Preferred weapon of the SAS." Keogh lifted

the Browning in one hand. "And the Parachute Regiment."

"He served with 1 Para," the girl said. "Bloody Sunday."

"Is that a fact?" Michael Ryan said.

"A long time ago. Lately I've been at sea."

"Belfast, but raised in London Kathleen tells me?"

"My mother died in childbirth. My father went to London in search of work. He's dead now."

Ryan had ejected the magazine from the butt of the Walther. "And a good Prod. You must be because of what you did for Kathleen."

"To be honest with you, religion doesn't mean a thing to me," Keogh told him. "But let's say I know which side I'm on."

At that moment, the door was flung open and a man in a cloth cap and raincoat rushed in, a revolver in one hand.

"Michael Ryan, you bastard, I've got you now," he cried and raised the revolver.

Ryan was caught, the magazine from the Walther on the table beside it. Keogh said, "What do I do, shoot him? All right. Bang, you're dead." He picked up the Browning and fired once. The man dropped the hand holding the revolver to one side. Keogh said, "Blanks, Mr. Ryan, I could tell by the weight. What kind of a game are we playing here?"

Ryan was laughing now. "Go on, Joseph, and get yourself a drink at the bar."

The supposed gunman turned away. The old men by the fire continued their card game as if nothing had happened.

Michael Ryan stood up. "Just a test, my old son, in a manner of speaking. Let's adjourn to the parlour and talk some more."

There was a fire in the grate of the small parlour, curtains drawn as rain drummed against the window. It was warm and comfortable and Ryan and Keogh sat opposite each other. The girl came in from the kitchen with a teapot, milk, and cups on a tray.

275

Ryan said, "If you're a seaman you'll have your papers."

"Of course," Keogh said.

Ryan held out his hand and Keogh shrugged, opened his reefer and took a wallet from his inside pocket.

"There you go. Ships' papers, union card, the lot."

The girl poured tea and Ryan examined everything closely. "Paid off the *Ventura* two weeks ago. Deck hand and diver. What's all that?"

"The *Ventura*'s a supply ship in the North Sea oilfields. Besides general ship's duties I did some diving. Not the really deep stuff. Just underwater maintenance, welding when necessary. That sort of thing."

"Interesting. A man of parts. Any special skills from the Parachute Regiment?"

"Just how to kill people. The usual weaponry skills. A considerable knowledge of explosives." Keogh lit a cigarette. "But where's all this leading?"

Ryan persisted. "Can you ride a motor cycle?"

"Since I was sixteen and that's a long time ago. So what?"

Ryan leaned back, took out a pipe and filled it from an old pouch. "Visiting relatives are you?"

"Not that I know of," Keogh said. "A few cousins scattered here and there. I came back on a whim. Nostalgia if you like. A bad idea really, but I can always go back and get another berth."

"I could offer you a job," Ryan said and the girl brought a taper from the fire to light his pipe.

"What, here in Belfast?"

"No, in England."

"Doing what?"

"Why, the kind of thing you did tonight. The kind of thing you're good at."

It was very quiet. Keogh was aware of the girl watching him eagerly. "Do I smell politics here?"

"Since nineteen sixty-nine I've worked for the Loyalist cause," Ryan said. "Served six years in the Maze prison. I hate Fenians. I hate the bloody Sinn Fein because if they win they'll drive us all out, every Protestant in the country. Ethnic cleansing to the hilt. Now if things get that bad

I'll take as many of them to hell with me as I can."

"So where's this leading?"

"A job in England. A very lucrative job. Funds for our organisation."

"In other words, we steal from someone," Keogh said.

"We need money, Keogh," Ryan said. "Money for arms. The bloody IRA have their Irish American sympathisers providing funds. We don't." He leaned forward. "I'm not asking you for patriotism. I'll settle for greed. Fifty thousand pounds."

There was a long pause and Ryan and the girl waited, her face sombre as if she expected him to say no.

Keogh smiled. "That's a lot of money, Mr. Ryan, so you'll be expecting a lot in return."

"Back-up is what I expect from a man who can handle anything and from the way you've carried yourself tonight you would seem to be that kind of man."

Keogh said, "What about your own people? You've as many gunmen out on the street as the IRA. More even. I know that from army days." He lit a cigarette and leaned back. "Unless there's another truth here. That you're in it for the money, you're in it for yourself."

Kathleen Ryan jumped up. "Damn you for saying that. My uncle has given more for our people than anyone I know. Better you get out of here while you can."

Ryan held up a hand. "Softly, child, any intelligent man would see it as a possibility. It's happened before, God knows and on both sides."

"So?" Keogh said.

"I can be as hungry as the next man where money is concerned, but my cause is a just one, the one certainty in my life. Any money that passes through my hands goes to the Protestant cause. That's what my life is about."

"Then why not use some of your own men?"

"Because people talk too much, a weakness in all revolutionary movements. The IRA have the same problem. I've always preferred to use what I call hired help and for that I go to the underworld. An honest thief who is working for wages is a sounder proposition that some revolutionary hothead."

"So that's where I come in?" Keogh said. "Hired help, just like anyone else you need?"

"Exactly. So, are you in or out? If it's no then say no. After what you did for Kathleen tonight you'll come to no harm from me."

"Well that's nice to know." Keogh shrugged. "Oh, what the hell, I might as well give it a try. A change from the North Sea. Terrible weather there at this time of the year."

"Good man yourself," Ryan smiled. "A couple of Bushmills, Kathleen, and we'll drink to it."